Fowler's

Folly

Cyberworld Publishing

Cyberworld Publishing

www.cyberworldpublishing.com

This book is copyright © 2015
Olivia Stowe asserts her right to be known as the author of this work.
First published by Cyberworld Publishing in 2015
Cover design by Cyberworld Publishing © 2015
Cover photo: Image manipulated: Copyright:scarfe@Depositphotos
E-book ISBN: 978-0-9943805-1-7
Paperback ISBN: 978-0-9943805-2-4
All rights reserved

Cyberworld Publishing
Jindalee St
Toronto, 2283 NSW
Australia

Fowler's Folly

Charlotte Diamond Mysteries Book 10

by

Olivia Stowe

Table of Contents

Chapter One: The Doorbell Rang

"It's all Charlotte's fault, of course. It's the curse of Charlotte."

"Chance!" his wife, Marilyn, exclaimed, "isn't it time you gave up that old family dig?"

The four of them, plus the family dogs, the Siberian husky, Sam, and the boxer, Rocket, were sitting in a semicircle in wooden Adirondack chairs behind Charlotte and Brenda's Federal-style plantation house on the banks of the Choptank River in the Maryland village of Hopewell on the Choptank. Chance, Charlotte's older brother, a doctor in Williamsburg, Virginia, and his United Methodist minister wife, Marilyn, had driven north to join them in preparing to go south again for a late-summer foursome vacation. They originally had planned to head to Hilton Head Island, South Carolina. The four of them had vacationed together a couple of years previously for a Christmas cruise down the Rhine and, most recently, for a wedding party cruise after Charlotte and Brenda were married. They had hit it off well as a traveling quartet, despite the adversity they'd all faced during these trips.

The kicker was that a hurricane, Charlie, had formed off the Florida coast and was projected to be passing over the South Carolina coast at the same time they planned to be at Hilton Head. The owner of the house they were renting had already called and strongly suggested they cancel.

"No, he's right," Charlotte said, turning a smile on her sister-in-law. "I've always had that effect."

"What effect?" Charlotte's spouse, Brenda, asked as she rose from her chair to pass around the chips and dip again. Both Sam and Rocket, who had been napping between their mistresses' chairs rose up on their haunches in hopeful anticipation of Brenda spilling the tray.

"Not a chance, chums," she said, with her signature tinkling laugh, known to moviegoers far and wide as that of the semiretired senior box-office star Brenda Brandon, although she was known in this village, where her family had lived for generations, as Brenda Boynton. In her new environment, she had grown accustomed to answering to either name, with those around her making the same adjustment.

With a "just for the record" whine from both of the pooches, they dutifully laid back down and dropped their muzzles on their forepaws. Being permitted to be out here with their people, who only recently had returned from an appearance by Brenda at the Spoleto music and theater festival in Charleston and a major drug bust south of there for Charlotte, both dogs were flying under the radar to the extent that they could. The dogs had been left behind. They knew if they didn't mind their manners, they'd be left behind again and stuck in the house with the housekeeper, Bea Helgerson. Not that the two dogs didn't love Bea, of course. They fully understood and appreciated that Bea would have continually let bits and pieces of delicious food drop to the floor for them in the kitchen, yet they still preferred to be out here was a testament to how much they loved their mistresses and wanted to be near them.

"I am the curse of East Coast vacations. Always have been," Charlotte said.

"I don't know how many times our family tried to take summer and fall vacations on the coast from Maine to Florida," Chance said, "But all of them were wiped out by hurricanes."

"*All* of them?" Brenda asked, incredulous.

"All that I can remember," Charlotte admitted, with a sigh. "Of course there's nothing like sitting through a hurricane on vacation to keep the experience in your memory."

"You were in the family too, Chance Diamond," his wife admonished. "Why blame it on Charlotte? Maybe the curse is yours. You're booked on this Hilton Head vacation too."

"You mean beside this one actually being named for Charlotte?" Chance countered.

They all laughed at the similarity of Charlotte's name to that of the hurricane, Charlie, that was threatening their vacation plans. The dogs perked up their ears and looked to the snack tray in the hope that the laughter was because it had spilled on the grass. But no such luck there.

"The family curse joke kept on going after I went out to California for Med school," Chance said, with a laugh. Looking directly at his wife, he said, "You know it happened when Charlotte was in college down at Elon and the family tried to include her in their beach vacations. You were at school with her. I seem to remember that on at least one of those occasions, you were invited to go along on a vacation wiped out by a hurricane. I was still out in California then."

"Well . . . ," Marilyn said, but then she couldn't think of anything else to say, so she piped down and dug into the chips and dip that a major box-office movie star was standing over her chair offering her.

"I guess we'll just have to bite the bullet and find somewhere else to go for the week—somewhere that we can get accommodations," Chance said. As the only man in the group, he felt compelled to take charge, although he was somewhat scared to do so in the face of a minister, a movie star, and his sister, Charlotte, a retired senior FBI agent of significant law and order reputation.

Or *was* she retired? he wondered. Brenda had just been telling them how Charlotte had been instrumental in breaking up a major drug ring down south of Charleston where cocaine in dime bags with a distinctive logo on them, a green palm tree, was being flown in by float plane and then distributed on north. It even had shown up right here at Curtain Call, the movie colony retirement community that Brenda and Charlotte had established just down the street.

Chance thought he needed to quickly establish someplace else for them to go, because Brenda had called him without telling Charlotte and asked him to set up this retreat. She was afraid that, even in retirement, Charlotte had been working too hard and needed a break. Charlotte was mayor of Hopewell, although that didn't take too much of her time, but she also had worked her derriere off in helping Brenda to establish the retirement complex, and now she had agreed to return part time to work with the Annapolis FBI office as a consultant.

"If not the coast and a hurricane, why don't we go to the mountains?" Chance declared, trying to sound as chipper as he could. "I don't think the hurricane will come far inland. The Poconos, in Pennsylvania, or maybe Asheville, North Carolina."

Marilyn sat up and gushed a, "Asheville would be great. The Grove Park Inn or the hotel recently built on the Biltmore estate would be spectacular. I've been wanting to see the Biltmore, and they've got a great arboretum there in Asheville. And Carl Sandburg's house is just south of there in Hendersonville. I can't think of much for us to do in the Poconos."

"I think we're too late to book at either of those hotels, Marilyn," he husband responded, "and I thought we'd agreed that we wanted something with a kitchen. But we should be able to find a short-term house or condo rental near Ashville if Brenda and Charlotte are happy with—"

He wasn't able to finish that thought, though, as Charlotte's cell phone was buzzing. When she rang off, she turned to the others with an apologetic look. "That was Evan Worthington," she said.

They didn't have to be told that; they all—including Sam and Rocket, who were sitting up and attentive—knew that Charlotte had been talking with the head agent of the Annapolis FBI office where Charlotte had worked before she retired. Evan also, not incidentally, had been a fervent suitor for Charlotte before Charlotte and Brenda had declared for each other and gotten married the previous winter right here in Hopewell on the heels of Maryland passing a same-sex marriage law. Evan had graciously backed off as a suitor—but not as an FBI office chief needing Charlotte to continue work as a consultant.

"And he wants you to stay here and work," Brenda said, the worry and dejection clear in her voice.

"Something like that," Charlotte answered. "I'm sure you know how important this would be. You were down in Charleston with me during the drug operation, and you know the havoc it caused here at Curtain Call. Evan says the packets of cocaine are turning up again—the same packet logo as we encountered in Charleston."

"It couldn't be ones left over from the earlier delivery, could it?" Chance asked.

"Maybe," Charlotte said, "but Evan doesn't think so. The transport route we uncovered has been shut down, and we assumed it would take them more time than this to develop a new route." She looked down at the two dogs, and Sam, sensing Charlotte was thinking about him, rose on his feet and trotted over to her to be petted. And in this he was right. Of course, when Sam was accepted and given attention, Rocket was there nosing in for pats too.

"When we came back from Charleston, I said we'd take the dogs next time—that we leave them here alone too much," Charlotte said. "I just don't know about going away from them again so soon. Maybe the hurricane is an omen for what I should do. Maybe I should stay here and the three of you should go on to Asheville."

"I'm not going on vacation without you," Brenda spoke up in a forceful voice. "Let's be clear about that. If you stay, I'll stay, and we'll rent a tent to stake out on the lawn and pretend we're vacationing."

Charlotte started to say something, but a dinner bell rang from within the house and they all gathered up the leavings of the cocktail hour and headed inside.

Brenda brushed the crumbs and last couple of crackers off the tray and onto the lawn where, getting the signal from her, the dogs gleefully inhaled the offering.

"Anyway, I vote for Asheville too," Charlotte said as they set out for the house, releasing much of the tension in the air, "so let's see what we can do down there as far as lodging that will accept the pups, and I'll see what I can do about getting away—at least part of the time."

* * * *

They were down to the coffee after the meal, having hashed out all of the possibilities and come around to Asheville again, when the doorbell rang. Marilyn, who was already up, having returned the coffee pot to the kitchen, where Bea was busy washing pots, went for the front door. Sam and Rocket sat up, curled their lips in unison, and each started a low growl. Charlotte instinctively reached for Sam's collar and Brenda for Rocket's. Chance rose and followed Marilyn toward the foyer.

12

The utterance of, "My god, is that you, Regina," brought Charlotte and Brenda to their feet, handing the dogs over to Bea, who had come into the dining room with their leashes, and moving to the entrance foyer in time to hear a disheveled woman say, "What the hell are you doing here, Marilyn? Where's Charlotte? I need Charlotte," and then collapse on the stoop. Looking past her through the open front door, they could see that she had run her big, black sedan, something that had escaped from some English lord's castle, up onto the lawn.

Marilyn knelt at the woman's side as Chance arrived and also knelt. Charlotte stood by, coffee cup and saucer in hand, and took a sip of her drink. Brenda was the last to arrive.

"Good grief, what is this all about?" Brenda asked. "Who is she, Charlotte? She said your name. She knows Marilyn."

"That's Regina Fowler," Charlotte said in a calm, almost disinterested voice. "An old college classmate of Marilyn and mine."

"I must say you're taking her appearance this way rather calmly," Brenda said.

"You of all people should be able to recognize theatrics when you see them," Charlotte answered. Her tone remained detached. "This is the way Regina has always made her appearances."

"Theatrics or not," Chance said, "the woman has fainted. Here, we should get her upstairs and on a bed. She feels feverish, as well." He started to raise the woman, with Marilyn's help, and with Brenda coming closer too, but the woman came alive enough to stand with just Chance's help.

"Please, no need to trouble yourselves. I'll just . . ." She let her voice fade away and she slumped against Chance. But it was evident that he could handle her alone and proceeded to guide her up the stairs to the bedroom level.

"You might recheck your medical license about being able to diagnose true fainting," Charlotte said.

"The back bedroom to the right should be fine," Brenda called up the staircase to Chance's and Regina's departing backs. When they were out of sight, she rounded on Charlotte. "I must say, Charlotte, you were a bit cold about that. She's obviously in distress and she asked specifically for you. What is going on with you two?"

Charlotte heaved a sigh and headed for the staircase. "Marilyn will fill you in. I suppose I will have to go upstairs and sort her out. You did consider that she's just drunk, I hope."

Brenda looked expectantly at Marilyn.

"Regina was, indeed, a classmate of ours at Elon. She was always hanging on Charlotte and both criticizing and trying to mimic her. And then a student from the nearby University of Virginia who Regina assumed was meant for her—wrongly, we all could see—started dating Charlotte, and Regina spent the rest of our senior year trying to make Charlotte's life a living hell. She tried to cover her tracks, but we all knew it was Regina."

"Fought over a man?" Brenda asked, amusement bleeding into her voice.

"Not fighting—at least me," Charlotte called out from half way up the staircase. "I had no idea he'd dated her first. And I should have just let her have him."

Charlotte was gone then and Brenda turned a questioning look at Marilyn.

"The man was Charlotte's eventual husband, Sydney," Marilyn said. "And every reference I've heard Charlotte make to Regina over the years was how she should have let Regina land Sydney—that they deserved each other."

* * * *

"So, I'm not hearing any explosions from upstairs," Marilyn said when Chance came back down to join Brenda and her at the table in the kitchen, where they were having another cup of coffee. They'd just waved good-bye to Bea, who wanted to check with her invalid aunt, Hannah, the village's self-proclaimed historian, across Hopewell on Spring street. As she often did at this time of night, Bea took Sam and Rocket with her to give them their evening exercise and "relief." On this particular evening, it was good she was around to do so, as neither Charlotte nor Brenda were mentally latched into the needs of their dogs just now. Brenda appeared to be lost in confusion.

"Is Regina sedated or asleep?" Brenda asked.

"She's quiet, not asleep but unresponsive," Chance answered. "Charlotte threw me out of the room. It was a blessing; I've had nightmares through life of being in a room together with those two. Although that's mainly because of Regina's outrageous behavior and scheming."

"So, you know this Regina too? Charlotte suggested she might be drunk."

"No, she isn't drunk. If this was caused by drink, I'd know it—I'd smell it on her for starters. But, this *is* vintage Regina."

"I've never seen Charlotte act this way before," Brenda said. "Were there really such problems between them—ones that lasted? If it was over Sydney, as we all know, Charlotte's been well over Sydney for a couple of years."

"It's not really Charlotte as much as it's Regina," Marilyn said, as she poured her husband a cup of coffee and he settled in at the table. "She drove all of us to distraction—not just Charlotte—with her hot and cold antics, and she's a little bit crazy and—"

"A *little* bit?" Chance interrupted. "You and Charlotte used to complain about the woman incessantly. More than a little bit crazy, you two always insisted. And I

15

could see it whenever I came in contact with her. Although she's probably the sanest one of the Fowler bunch."

"The Fowler bunch?" Brenda asked, still wide-eyed.

"It's down to three cousins now, I think. All women," Chance said. "Regina's the middle one in age. The older one's named Samantha and the younger is Clea. All from different mothers descended from a shared great grandfather—Franklin Fowler, if I remember rightly—and all living in that big, moldering castle on top of the Blue Ridge. What's the place called, Marilyn?"

"Fowler's Folly."

"Yes, that's it."

"Strange name," Brenda said, taking on a pensive look, "but a familiar one. I suppose there's a story behind the house and the family."

"There sure is," Chance said. He cocked his ear to see if he could hear raised voices from the upper floor or Charlotte's footsteps on the stairs, but hearing nothing that might need a referee, he settled in to bringing Brenda up to speed on their unexpected house guest.

"The Fowler patriarch early in the twentieth century, Franklin Fowler, was a munitions manufacturer in Richmond. At one time—before his factory blew up and he and Clea's grandmother were killed in a train wreck when vacationing out West; Arizona, I think—his operation rivaled that of the DuPonts up in Delaware. The family had a huge estate on the James just west of Richmond, with the munitions factory between the estate and the city limits. Like most wealthy Richmond families, the original Fowler couple wanted to retreat to the cooler, less mosquito-infested, mountains during the summer. The Blue Ridge mountains are only about eighty miles west of Richmond. Apparently there eventually were three wives, forming three branches downward. Samantha's grandmother, the first Mrs. Fowler, Claudia, was a celebrated beauty but also what they then called 'delicate in disposition.' Until recently politically correct days this typically was called 'crazier than a loon.' One story behind building a house in the Blue Ridge was that Franklin Fowler wanted to get her out of Richmond as much as possible."

"Oh," Brenda said, looking away from the table.

"Oh, what?" Chance asked. "You heard this story before."

"Don't mind me," Brenda said in a slightly remote voice. "Go on, I want to hear this. You seem to be well versed on the place."

Chance continued. "I'd heard snatches of the story before and a couple of weeks ago, I got an investor's prospectus about buying up the place and making it into a hotel with a golf course. That sent me to the Internet to find out more about it. Anyway, so, Franklin Fowler spent twenty years building an Italianate monstrosity, with square towers and everything, at the top of the Blue Ridge, near where the Wintergreen Resort is now—above Charlottesville in the Piedmont to the northeast and the Shenandoah Valley to the west. He had a miniature version of the bigger mansion built that they called the replica house, and that's where they actually lived, because Fowler went nearly bust from the factory explosion and he and his last wife died before the house was completed enough to occupy.

"The family has managed to hold onto it, though, and, as I recall, everyone in the family has retained the family name. I know Regina has. Samantha's father was some sort of spiritualism guru and was running a spiritualism colony and school on the property when we knew Regina at Elon. I don't know if that's still running. I did hear that both of Samantha's parents had died—the father in the last few years. The colony actually gained more publicity, I think, when Samantha's brother took it over for a short while. I think he came back to it from something in show business."

17

"What a strange—but appropriate name—Fowler's Folly," Brenda said.

"It wasn't originally named that," Marilyn interjected. "I think it originally was called Fowler's Retreat. But then there were so many tragedies that the name eventually got changed."

"Tragedies?" Brenda asked. "There was the factory explosion that halted construction and Fowler and his wife dying in the train wreck, but . . ."

"It wasn't just the manner of death of the third Mrs. Fowler," Marilyn said. "The other two had bad ends too—and although the Fowler women tend to be long lived, the Fowler men die young or tragically. I understand that Samantha's brother committed suicide for unrequited love or something like that. Very theatrical."

"Now I remember about Samantha's father," Chance said. "Shot in his study, reportedly a suicide too, but there seems to have been some question of that."

"And the first two wives of the patriarch?" Brenda asked. She wasn't looking at them now, but staring off in space as if having seen the kitchen wallpaper for the first time.

"I told you there was a miniature version of the castle. I understand that the first Mrs. Fowler, the one said to be off her rocker, was living there full time—not going back to Richmond in the fall—and actually was restrained in that replica house. The house burned down, with her in it. Legend has it that she burned it herself. And Fowler never again went up there. His family still went up for part of the summers and camped out in the uncompleted castle. The second Mrs. Fowler fell to her death from one of the towers of the main house. That's when the papers coined the name Fowler's Folly, and it stuck."

"Fascinating," Brenda said. "Sounds like it would make a good movie plot. I'd like to see the place."

Marilyn and Chance could see the wheels spinning in the movie star's mind. She had the clout still in Hollywood to get such a movie made if she wanted. The doctor and his wife knew that the production crew and acting ensemble she had often worked with were pressing her to do another movie. Her ensemble included her own out-of-wedlock son, Tony Trice, born of a teenage affair shortly before Brenda went to Hollywood and took it by storm. She'd been telling her colleagues she hadn't seen a script that would lure her back. They could see that she had stars in her eyes now, though. She had been trying to retire fully over the past two years, and her Hollywood colleagues had managed to pull her back for another movie and even for concert appearances.

"And these three female cousins have always lived together in isolation on that mountaintop. I wonder?" Brenda asked in a voice that sounded like her mind was in another realm, weaving a movie script.

"The youngest—Clea—has always lived there, I think," Marilyn said. "She swallowed the spiritualism bit hook, line, and sinker, I believe, and became one of the attractions for the spiritualist colony. The older sister, Samantha, was gone from there the longest, it seems. She was an international journalist and lived abroad for many years before coming back to Virginia. I don't recall there ever having been a husband. And Regina got a finance degree at Elon College while Charlotte and I were there too and went on to work in New York for a while."

"You seemed to have kept track of them," Brenda said.

"I was class secretary and Regina talked about her family quite freely. I'm the class contact point for alumnae, and she gives me a rundown on the family each time I send out a contact letter or updating e-mail. And I'll admit I'm fascinated by the house and family, and the legend. I'd like to see the place too," Marilyn said. "With all those tragedies, it certainly must be haunted. Regina often talked about it when we were at college, and she'd tease us about inviting us up there for a weekend. But she never did. I hear it has a gigantic Tiffany window in the stair hall, a portrait in stained glass of Samantha's grandmother, who Regina always said, rather bitterly, was a great beauty of her day even if she sank into insanity."

"There's another legend about the place," Chance said. When the others turned their heads to him, he continued. "The usual buried gold story about such piles of marble in unusual places. Franklin supposedly was still very rich when he died in that train crash, but very few assets other than Fowler's Folly and the crippled munitions factory were found. So, naturally, speculation is that there's a fortune hidden in a secret compartment at Fowler's Folly. There have periodically been reports of vandalism in search of the treasure that have been associated with the story—none of which has helped the family in maintaining the place."

Just then Charlotte reappeared, went to the kitchen counter to pour herself another cup of coffee, and joined the other three at the table. "Sorry about that," she said. "Regina just is always able to get to me."

"Is she awake? Have you talked with her?" Marilyn asked.

"She won't admit she's awake, but I think she's playing possum. If she was the cousin descended from Samantha's grandmother instead of Samantha, her behavior wouldn't surprise me a bit. I guess it will be morning before—"

With a screech, Regina, now dressed in a bathrobe and little else, careened into the room, went directly to Charlotte, and clutched at her with claws. "You must come up to the Folly, Charlotte. You must help us. Something evil is being unleashed."

"Why?" Charlotte asked. "And just stop this nonsense and tell us what you want without all of these silly histrionics. What can I possibly do to help you?"

"You're FBI," Regina said—more like screeched, "I've heard you work for the FBI. You can stop this without there being any prison. You must help us with . . . with this." She tossed something onto the table, but no one saw what it was immediately. They were all trying to get her under control. At this point, though, she just collapsed into Chance's arms.

"I'll take her back upstairs," he said.

"We'll discuss this in the morning when you're not as hysterical," Charlotte said.

Regina didn't fight Chance as he guided her back to the foyer and the stairs to the second floor.

"Has she always been this . . . dramatic?" Brenda asked, when the three women were alone again.

"Yes, always," Charlotte and Marilyn responded simultaneously, and then both nervously laughed, recognizing that this was a more pathetic than amusing situation.

And then, looking at the table, Charlotte said, "Shit."

"What?" Brenda asked.

Charlotte picked up what Regina had thrown on the table—a dime packet filled with a white powder substance. There was a logo on the packet in green ink. A palm tree.

"I should have known," Charlotte said, with a sigh. "What do you want to bet that's cocaine in the packet? Guess I'll have to go upstairs and get her to talk."

Once more she threw Chance out of the bedroom. Once more he was glad to be relieved. But this time, when he was downstairs and had been asked, he said, "Regina's as lucid as she's likely to get. The two of them are talking now."

When Charlotte came downstairs, she paused in the doorway. "Where'd I put my cell phone? I wonder whether it's too late to call Evan."

"I doubt that any time would be too late for Evan if you call him," Brenda said. Charlotte shot a look at her spouse, but there didn't seem to be a bit of purposeful irony in what Brenda said. Brenda knew Evan had wanted Charlotte and still would want her if she were free—which she wasn't. But Brenda, eternally even tempered and trustful, had never shown jealousy or competitiveness toward Evan. "What's up? What did you learn from Regina?"

"I learned that I have to go up to Fowler's Folly after the dinner at Elon College. The rest of you can go on to Asheville if you like—but Regina has invited us all up to the castle. And I, at least, will have to go. Evan will want me to go to find out what the connection is between the Fowlers and these drugs."

"We're invited too?" Marilyn asked.

"Yes, all of us, if we want to go."

"Well, hot diggedty," Marilyn exclaimed. "Count me in. I've always wanted to see the place. Let's spend our vacation there, Chance."

Chance didn't look all that enthusiastic, but it already was two to one. He turned and looked quizzically at Brenda.

"I wouldn't miss it for all the world," Brenda said. Her voice seemed more distant than amused—or even enthusiastic, for that matter.

Charlotte shot her a questioning look, but Brenda was looking like she was living in the past. Knowing how worried Charlotte was about the pull of Hollywood on Brenda, neither Marilyn nor Chance mentioned what Brenda had said about the legend of Fowler's Folly being a good movie storyline or provided the explanation that she probably already was weaving plots, costumes, and settings.

"That's it then," Charlotte said. "Asheville is out and Fowler's Folly is in. There's only one really good thing about all of this."

"What's that?" Brenda, who could see something good about it that she knew Charlotte couldn't see yet, asked.

"Sam and Rocket can go with us on this vacation. Regina says they are invited too."

* * * *

"I'm sorry, this isn't the vacation you had planned on."

Charlotte and Brenda were in a close embrace on their bed. Mellow from winding down together from the evening's surprise event and the double change in where they were headed for the next week.

"It's fine for me," Brenda responded, kissing Charlotte on the throat. They had just, for the third time, directed Sam and Rocket back to their individual dog beds across the room from the master bed. "I find the Fowler Folly story fascinating. And the Fowler name is familiar. I suppose you've referred to Regina before in our conversations and now I can put a background to that."

"I've talked about Regina as little as possible since I left Elon. You might be familiar with the name because Regina's aunt was connected with the movies and is one of our residents at the retirement village."

"Hortense Fowler, the former personal assistant to the director Otto Frantz, is one of those Fowlers?"

"Yes. She's been here, what? A little more than a year? She's been doing her clairvoyant act at Curtain Call for nearly that long, I'm sure. She's a little off."

"Now, Charlotte, she must be over a hundred. We'll both be mumbling in our porridge when we get to that age."

"Me, yes. You, no. but it doesn't matter if we are as long as we're still together. Anyway, Hortense is a Fowler through and through. There are times when I think that Regina is as batty as her aunt is."

"The family sounds delicious. I can't wait to see the place."

"You're already looking at it in terms of a movie plot, aren't you?" Charlotte murmured.

"You know me too well. Do you mind terribly?"

"Not terribly. And how can I complain? I'll be there on business. And I know you've wanted me to get away from it all on this vacation."

"It's not your fault there's a hurricane coming up the coast," Brenda said.

"Apparently it is," Charlotte answered. "Chance already explained that to you."

Both women laughed, and Brenda reached over and turned out the nightlight. "As long as it's what you want."

"I want these bags of cocaine with the palm logo to stop coming into the country," Charlotte answered.

"You've never felt that case was closed, have you?" Brenda asked with a sigh.

"I originally did. I thought we had them all tied up neatly, until another float plane came in with drugs after we left."

"But they apprehended that man too—a seasoned criminal—didn't they? What was his name?"

"Jason Gordon."

"Yes, Gordon. A wanted murderer. Sent to prison down in Georgia, wasn't he, but escaped a few months ago?"

"Yes, knowing he's on the loose—although he probably headed straight for South America—keeps me concerned about that case. And him showing up in Charleston, with a planeload of drugs, when we thought we'd settled the case, made me wonder if there weren't even more couriers. Now we're finding the drugs in the region again. So, yes, the worry we haven't completely closed that case is ever in the back of my mind. But for right now, you know what I want."

"What *we* want," Brenda murmured, as she moved her body over Charlotte's.

Later, in the dark of the night, both women spent and now breathing regularly, Sam and Rocket quietly left their beds, padded over to their mistresses' bed, and jumped onto the mattress as lightly as they could manage. As usual, they both wanted to move into the warmth between the two women's bodies. But, as usual, the two women were still in an embrace, and there wasn't an inch of space between them for a dog—certainly not a dog of the size of either the husky or the boxer—to wedge in. With a contented sigh, knowing they'd made it this far, both settled down against each other at the foot of the bed.

Maybe before one of the women woke in the morning the dogs would manage to get off the bed and back to their own. But, then maybe not. If they didn't, there would be a scolding. But it would be delivered with a smile. The two women spoiled the dogs rotten.

Chapter Two: The Sinking College

Realizing that having taken two days spinning wheels over what to do about the hurricane threatening their Hilton Head Island vacation had foreshortened their preparations to leave now that they had switched gears, Charlotte and Brenda got up before the rest of the house woke and even before Bea Helgerson arrived to make breakfast. Changing their destination could have allowed them to set their vacation dates back, but they were due at an alumnae dinner at Charlotte and Marilyn's undergraduate college, Elon, in the town by the same name, near Lynchburg in Virginia on Friday, so they had to keep to the original schedule. They hurriedly wolfed down muffins and inhaled coffee and then put Sam and Rocket on leashes for a walk up River Street toward the peninsula jutting into the Choptank River where Curtain Call was located.

Just as she was trying to retire to her ancestral home in Hopewell on the Choptank from a thunderously successful movie career—so thunderous that Brenda had become weary of it—she both was at loose ends on how to redirect her life and won multiple millions of dollars that she didn't really need in the Maryland lottery. Two other momentous events had occurred to her at that point. First, she met and quickly became close to Charlotte Diamond, and, second, she decided that her future calling would be to establish a most-fees-underwritten retirement home in Hopewell for those who had worked in the movie industry. Charlotte had bought into the plan and moved into Brenda's house when her own riverside cottage on River Street became encapsulated in the grounds of Curtain Call.

The previous Christmas, with the passage of the same-sex marriage law in Maryland, the two tied the knot in the village's Episcopal church in a blinding snowstorm.

On the morning after the dramatic appearance of Regina Fowler at their home, Charlotte had the sensation that there was something out of kilter when they left the house and turned south. But the dogs were straining at their leashes and trying their best to entangle their mistresses in them, and that's where her concentration went. Neither of the women were thrilled to have to be out and about that early—mainly needing to meet with Curtain Call's lawyer, Chuck Dawson, on a bequest left to the retirement home by a former resident.

There was money coming to Curtain Call from Betty Bentley, a former movie actress who had once seen herself on the level of Brenda Brandon—but of course she never was. Always seeing herself as being due more respect at Curtain Call as a resident, and maybe even more than the owner and benefactress Brenda Brandon herself, Betty had been one of the original set of what was termed "The Terribles"—an attrition-revolving quartet of sourpusses in residence who couldn't be pleased by anything that was being done for them and who combined their complaints to sing them in harmony. Whenever one of The Terribles bowed out of life, he or she was quickly and mysteriously replaced by another champion complainer and schemer. Surprisingly, Betty had left her money to Curtain Call—she had really no one else to leave it to—but, as a last dig at the retirement community's administration, she'd put in the stipulation that the money had to go to one big bash so "the community at last could have something worthwhile and entertaining done for them."

Brenda and Charlotte had to meet with Chuck Dawson before they went anywhere on vacation to pin down what this project would be or else the money was going to go to a cancer charity that recently had been exposed as siphoning nearly all of the funds off into high administration salaries.

Charlotte had half a notion to let the money go there, but Brenda, ever cheerful and sunny, was sure they could find something to do with it to benefit the Curtain Call residents. They were still discussing that point as they reached the front door of the retirement home, to find a rest home's version of pandemonium in the day room and spilling out into the front foyer in the guise of facility staffers moving briskly about, cajoling residents, and residents either shuffling or wheeling for the corridors leading away from the public areas. The home was built like spokes of a wheel, the residents' commodious suites radiating out from the central public areas. With the shores of the Choptank River on two sides and a lagoon on a third, all of the residential units had a view of water.

Brenda stood back, somewhat bemused at the unexpected flurry of activity, while Charlotte put out a hand to stay the brisk passage of one of the home's nurse's aides, Sally Fortness.

"What's the commotion about, Sally?" she asked.

"I'm afraid it's Miss Fowler again," Sally answered. "She's gone into her fortuneteller routine again in the middle of the day room—which of course the residents love, having forgotten about previous times, and she's causing panic."

"Panic?" Brenda asked. "How so?"

"She tells everyone they're about to die. Some of the women residents have fainted, and the men are all getting belligerent."

Just then, the home administrator, Evonne Clagett, a small bundle of flaming redheaded activity and competence, arrived. "Brenda. Charlotte. Thank goodness you're here— and you've brought Sam and Rocket. The boys are needed in the day room stat."

Neither Brenda nor Charlotte needed a translation for this. There was nothing more soothing for the elderly residents in the retirement home than a visitation by dogs or cats. Indeed, it was to provide such a treat—as well as that the dogs wouldn't have let them leave the house without providing a morning walk—that the women had brought them along. Sam and Rocket enjoyed the visits as much as the residents did. The two women went into action.

"I'll take on Hortense," Charlotte said to Brenda. "You get the boys inserted in the milling crowd. Between their favorite actress and Sam and Rocket, you should be able to reestablish order, while I distract Hortense and neutralize her."

"Sounds like a plan," Brenda and Evonne said in unison.

"I'll get snacks cranked up early," Evonne said, as she pulled Sally Fortness away to help her.

"Now there, hello Hortense," Charlotte said as she moved into position at the small round table across from where the old, weathered and gaunt, but still somewhat regal and patrician-looking woman was sitting in her wheelchair. She had a scarf, with gold coins dangling from it, covering her head, which put her in her fortuneteller mode. An old man had just lurched off from the chair Charlotte slid her considerable bulk into. The expression on his face and that he was covering his heart with his hand as he struggled away indicated that Hortense had given yet another resident a warning of immediately impending doom.

"I'm so pleased that you are giving fortunes again today," Charlotte said. "I haven't had mine told for a while."

Hortense took Charlotte's hand, opened her palm, and stared into it intently. "I see jagged lines—look at these—at these jagged lines."

Charlotte looked. "Yep, they look jagged, and that means—?"

Not directly answering her, Hortense gave a little cry and then, in hushed tones. "And your life line. Abruptly cut. I'm sorry to say—"

"We all die at some point, Hortense," Charlottes said, causing the old woman to deflate in the theatrics she was building up to. "So, doesn't everyone have a cut life line? If not, they never can die?"

The old woman pulled herself up into her most patrician stance. "Yes, but not cut as close to the beginning of the line as this. And those jagged lines . . . well, I don't know if you want to know about those."

Charlotte looked around the day room. It only slowly was settling down to normal, although Brenda and the dogs were having their beneficial effect and she could see down the corridor past the dining room and toward the kitchens that Evonne and Sally were approaching with refreshments.

"Of course I want to know about those," she said.

"They speak of danger—of attempts on your life— and I'm afraid with the foreshortened life line—"

"They aren't a surprise. I've lived a life of danger, in the FBI, almost since college. Which reminds me. Regina, your niece, is in town—at our house—we'll have her come visit you this—"

"Regina? Here?" Hortense hissed, her face suddenly becoming contorted, and her wheelchair pulling away from the table. "No wonder. No wonder about the jagged lines. You must be careful . . . very careful . . . Charlotte

Diamond. Regina? No . . . I should have known. And keep that witch away from me."

With that, the woman had backpedaled from the table and was wheeling off toward the door into the foyer, leaving Charlotte sitting there, looking at the woman's hasty retreat with her jaw dropped.

Brenda came over, looking amused. "Well, whatever you said to Hortense was effective in getting her out of here. What did you say?"

"Nothing, really. Just that Regina Fowler was in town and we'd bring her by to see Hortense."

"Apparently Hortense doesn't particularly like that idea," Brenda said, adding on her signature tinkling laugh, which had several residents nearby laughing with her in response even though they didn't have a clue why they were laughing other than that Brenda's laugh was highly contagious.

"No she doesn't," Charlotte said. "But there isn't anything surprising in that, I guess. I've often wanted to run out of the room screaming when Regina's name came up in conversation—and especially at the suggestion of a possible Regina visitation. All seems quiet on the Curtain Call front now. Shall we get the meeting with Chuck over with, go home, and get Regina up and out?"

Speaking of Regina, as the quartet of Brenda, Charlotte, Sam, and Rocket approached the old Federal-style plantation house north on River Street that Brenda had inherited and restored, Charlotte realized what had bothered her as they left the house.

Last night Regina's car had been parked haphazardly up on the lawn. This morning it hadn't been there. It wasn't in the driveway either.

When they got into the house, Marilyn and Chance were still at the kitchen table, drinking coffee and chatting with Bea Helgerson as she puttered about.

"Where's Regina? Isn't she up yet?" Charlotte asked, as they came into the room and Sam and Rocket went to each of those in the kitchen for a greeting of assurance from the humans they were responsible for before settling down in their dog beds.

"She isn't with you?" Chance asked. "She was gone and her bed made when Marilyn and I got up."

"No, and her car's gone—it was gone when Brenda and I left the house before seven."

"Well, that's Regina for you," Marilyn said, taking an unconcerned swig of her coffee. "Unexpectedly dropping in on stage and just as unexpectedly departing after having stirred the pot. I'm just glad her brand of theatrics didn't stretch over days. We really need to be getting everything in order so we can get on the road. Did your meeting with your lawyer work out OK?"

"Yes, fine," Brenda said, "although we have to think fast on what to do for the residents with this bequest money. The place was somewhat in an uproar this morning. I thought the residents would really be upset, but I talked to one of the men in passing, and he said they hadn't had such entertaining excitement in months. He seemed downright giddy and invigorated—which gave Evonne Clagett the nub of an idea for how to spend the money."

"How's that?" Chance asked.

"She noted that Christmas time is the roughest time of year for the elderly and infirm. It's a family and friends holiday and some people have just about run out of those. And it's a destination holiday. People who are ill often hold out to make it to Christmas and then die soon thereafter. It's the time of year that we lose the most residents. So, Evonne suggested that we do something big at Christmas to take the residents' minds off the dangers and sadness of the season. With that in mind that's how we're planning to spend the money—although I don't yet know how."

"I have some ideas on that," Charlotte said, but she didn't follow up on what they were at the moment. She was too distracted by what Hortense had said. Hortense obviously hadn't been pleased with the appearance of Regina. Neither was Charlotte, but she'd already committed to going up to Fowler's Folly at Regina's insistence. And she'd already told Evan Worthington that there may be a connection between Fowler's Folly and the drug transportation case the FBI was concentrating on and that Charlotte—and Brenda—had already become embroiled in on their last trip south, to Charleston.

Charlotte just wished that the flighty Regina Fowler wasn't involved in all of this.

* * * *

Looking past Charlotte, through the open front door and down the front steps of the columned porch of the Magnolia House B&B between Charlottesville and Amherst, the gaunt older man with the flowing gray mane, and a stiff back that made him look like a Civil War general for the south, gave Charlotte an imperial look. That he'd said his name was Colonel Forest only added to the aura he exuded. "You reserved two rooms with queen-sized beds, right?" he said, looking at the registration form Charlotte filled out. "A couple and two women. We do have some singles, but alas only one of them—"

"Yes, two double rooms," Charlotte answered, knowing that the colonel had looked beyond her to confirm that there were three women and one man in their party. Chance was pulling luggage out of the back of his car. Marilyn was standing away from the car, holding the sniffing Sam and Rocket on leashes. What had determined the accommodations they'd picked for the night in Amherst had been the fact that this B&B had a very nice kennel and dog run attached to it. Brenda was still picking and

33

choosing from the interior of Chance's Avalon what she thought she'd needed to take to their rooms.

"Two married couples. Doctor and Doctor Diamond"—she knew this would set Colonel Forest on his heels—"and my spouse and me. I'm Charlotte Diamond and she's Brenda Boynton." Charlotte could have used Brenda's stage name, but she wasn't in the mood for that.

It didn't matter if she was in a mood for it or not, though. The B&B's host let a very brief look of distaste and judgment cross his face—one that Charlotte knew full well from when she and Brenda traveled in the true South and outside the urban areas—but then his face lit up as Brenda, all famous smiles, started mounting the stairs to the front door.

"My, she looks like. That wouldn't be . . . would it?"

"I imagine it is, yes," Charlotte said, "Boynton is the name she uses outside of the movies." And then she almost wanted to say something else to the old coot when, star struck, he did a complete about face, hustled to the door, and unctuously welcomed the movie star Brenda Brandon to his humble inn.

Back with just Charlotte for the necessary sign-ins as, mint juleps in hand, Brenda and the Doctors Diamond had been ushered into the front parlor, the colonel said, "Are you here for the alumnae dinner for those trying to save Elon College?"

"Yes," Charlotte answered.

"It's a pity about the closing of the college," he said, genuine regret in his voice. Charlotte could understand that. The college was the bread and butter for this community. And, as if he'd heard her thoughts, he continued. "Elon has been everything to this town for over a hundred years. I don't know how we will survive without it."

"Perhaps it won't close," she said. "There are many of us with very fond memories of our time here. Perhaps we can help keep it open. I suppose the area is swarming with alumnae. Mrs. Diamond and I both went to Elon, but we're just stopping here to take in the dinner and show our support on our way up to the mountain—to a place called Fowler's Folly. Above the Wintergreen resort."

"Ah, yes, the Fowlers," the colonel said, his voice a little tight.

"You know the Fowlers?"

"Oh, yes, they've been very active in Elon College affairs. Two of them have recently served on the board of visitors. I believe one of our Ms. Fowler guests is still on the board. I don't know if she's trying to close the school down or save it, though."

"Regina Fowler is staying at this B&B?" Charlotte asked, feeling a horror that she hoped she wasn't conveying.

"Oh, no, ma'am. She doesn't stay here. Nothing is good enough for that woman in these parts other than the Lee-Jackson resort over by Lynchburg. No, it's an older Fowler, Ms. Samantha, who is staying here."

Charlotte thanked him and, mint julep in hand, went into the parlor to deliver the bad news. One Fowler cousin was much the same as another in terms of not wanting to meet up with them. It was only then that she realized, with a groan, that she had signed up to take a vacation under the noses of all three of them up at Fowler's Folly.

Not more than ten minutes later their host walked back into the parlor with reverent steps and a look of deep awe on his face.

"Excuse me, Ms. Diamond?"

"Yes," Charlotte and Marilyn said in unison, turning toward him.

"Ms. Charlotte Diamond," he said hesitatingly, looking at Charlotte with a strange look that seemed somehow between disbelief and renewed respect. Charlotte inclined her head in a signal that he had her attention.

"There's a telephone call for you. You can take it in my office off the front hall. It's . . . it's President Chafin."

"Margaret Chafin?" Charlotte asked. Margaret Chafin was the acting president of Elon College, the former one having resigned in disgust on having been given two-weeks' notice that the board of visitors was closing the school down for financial reasons. Margaret Chafin had also been Charlotte's philosophy professor when Charlotte had been at the college. She didn't remember, however, having been one of Professor Chafin's favorite pupils.

Now what? she thought. "Thank you, can you show me to your phone?"

"Certainly, madam," Colonel Forest answered, still in awe. Charlotte understood. The president of the college would be regarded as a goddess by businessmen in the town of Elon. He ushered her to the phone like she was royalty.

* * * *

"It was good of you to see me like this," Margaret Chafin said after she'd opened the passenger door of the Avalon and slid into the seat next to Charlotte. "Like this" was quite cloak and dagger, both women driving to the parking lot behind a local, closed public library, and President Chafin leaving her car for Chance's, which Charlotte had borrowed for this rendezvous. Charlotte was dressed for the alumnae dinner being held in the local Holiday Inn ballroom, as it wasn't an event that could be held at the college. President Chafin was not dressed for a formal dinner.

"I won't keep you long," she went on to say. "I know you have a dinner to go to. I'm sure you realize that I can't go to the dinner, although of course my sentiments are with those trying to keep the college open."

36

"Yes, I understand," Charlotte answered. In fact, she understood quite well. The whole situation was dicey. Suddenly in March, the board of visitors of the prestigious women's college, which had opened in 1901—one of the only women-only liberal arts colleges still running in the South—had announced that this would be the last year for graduation at Elon, that the doors would be closed in August, leaving all of the undergraduates as well as the faculty members high and dry. It was too late in the school year for the students to apply for admission or the teachers and staff employment at other colleges for the coming year. The board said that, financially, the school could not continue into another year and that enrollment, then at seven hundred, had been steadily declining over the past decade. Its endowment was down to $84 million. The board was divided, but those in favor of closing the institution were in the majority.

The college president had promptly resigned in protest, and Margaret Chafin, a long-time professor and department head, had been appointed to fill the slot until the buildings shuttered their doors in August. Her primary role since then, she'd told Charlotte over the telephone, was to place the five hundred and some abandoned undergraduates in other colleges. Several colleges had stepped up to reopening their admissions programs. She also was doing what she could to reassign faculty members. She herself could retire, but she hadn't planned to. The college had been her life.

"If I showed any solidarity with the alumnae who are trying to keep the college open, I'd be dismissed on the spot. The board doesn't seem that concerned about placing the undergraduates or in finding new jobs for the faculty. I don't think the board anticipated the backlash it's gotten or the strength and determination of the alumnae in opposing the closing. The alumnae have gotten a temporary restraining order and have dug up the original endowment papers, which are in the form of a trust. The board had assumed they could follow corporate law in divesting, but apparently that isn't possible with a trust. None of the endowment money can be spent on closing costs; it all would have to go back to the heirs of the founder. Learning this was a double-edged sword. A couple of the heirs are on the board and have switched their votes from opposing closing to supporting it."

"I can see your predicament and the need for secrecy in speaking with any alumnae in opposition to the closure, but I don't understand why you wanted to meet with me."

"I've followed your career, Charlotte. You were always one of my favorite students and I was fascinated by your decision to pursue a career as an FBI agent when you graduated. That seemed so refreshing in the paternalistic world we lived in at the time." This was all news to Charlotte—that Chafin even remembered Charlotte had been in classes she taught—but she wanted to know what this was all about and there wasn't much time before she had to pick up the others to go to the dinner, so she didn't interrupt. "I know you rose up the ranks in the FBI and have become a top-notch investigator."

"You make me blush, Professor, but—"

"I need your investigation talents, Charlotte. If the college's endowment really was $84 million, we probably could survive and continue to operate—especially with the awakening among the alumnae of the danger we're in and the willingness they are showing to contribute to keep us open. But we don't really have an $84 million endowment. The board is trying to keep it hush-hush, but a big part of the endowment has disappeared."

"Disappeared? How much?" Charlotte asked.

"A bit over $20 million. I would like your help in trying to figure out where it went. The board seems more intent on hiding that its gone and making it just go away as a problem in the divestment. But I'd like to try to recover it so that we can stay open until the alumni have had a chance to organize to put us on solid financial ground. Besides, the records say we have $84 million, and that's what the heirs would expect to be returned to them if the school closes."

"I'd like to help, but I'm only here for tonight. And I'm off with my party tomorrow for a vacation that isn't completely a vacation. I'm on a bit of assignment. Perhaps when I've finished that—"

"You're going to the Blue Ridge, I understand. To Fowler's Folly."

"Yes, but how did you know that?"

"Samantha Fowler is on the board now and Regina was on the board before her. I saw Regina today and she told me you were going up to Fowler's Folly."

So Regina really is here, Charlotte thought. Shit. But, "Yes, that's right," is what she said, hoping the woman wasn't a mind reader. "So I'll be out of commission for—"

"We have no idea who managed to take the money, but it had to be someone on or connected with the board. Until we know otherwise, it could be one or both of the Fowler cousins. I'd like you to try to rule them out. It shouldn't be too difficult to discern whether either is benefiting from a financial windfall. I've known the Fowlers for years. It's all they've been able to do to keep that pile of granite up there standing. They likely are desperate for money. Just let me know if one or both of them could have our missing $20 million."

The request seemed reasonable enough to Charlotte. She couldn't say no. And she wouldn't put it past either Samantha or Regina to have tried to pull this embezzlement off.

* * * *

Most in the ballroom of the Holiday Inn that evening had reason to think the dinner was a great success and hope was high for saving the college. The state supreme court had just intervened and put the divestiture on hold, useful ideas were being thrown out, committees of influential alumnae were being formed, and pledges of money to both the defense and endowment funds were mounting.

Charlotte was perhaps the only one who was in deep consternation almost from the beginning of the meal—and that had nothing to do with the status of the college. Her companions, Brenda, Marilyn, and Chance, were concerned as well.

Samantha and Regina Fowler were both there, although sitting about as far away from each other as the room allowed. That wasn't the real problem, though. When Regina entered the room—late, of course, and parading like she was the spring princess, which she had been her senior year at Elon—Charlotte's attention snapped not to Regina but to her escort.

"That's Sydney," she exclaimed.

"So it is," Brenda said, too shocked to add to that.

"Shouldn't he be in prison?" Chance said.

"As far as I know they never caught him," Charlotte muttered.

Escorting Regina Fowler into the room was Sydney Morrison, Charlotte's deadbeat and perpetually scheming former husband in Annapolis until he ran off with his secretary, Gloria. This event had led to Charlotte's decision to retire from the FBI, completely reorder her life, and move to one of leisure and seclusion that thus far had proved to be anything but that in Hopewell on the Choptank. The reference to prison was because Sydney's scheme after splitting with Charlotte was to open up a casino in Ocean City, Maryland, by selling well over 100 percent of the shares to unwitting investors that included not only Brenda but also Gloria's relatives, who turned out to be New Jersey mobsters. The last Charlotte knew, Sydney and Gloria were on the lam not only from the Feds but also from the New Jersey mafia.

But here he was, in Elon, Virginia, squiring Regina Fowler, who he had dated before he met and married Charlotte.

Regina made sure that Charlotte knew he was there. She trotted him by the Diamonds' table—somewhat reluctantly on Sydney's part—and hesitated there.

"I think you've met my husband, Sydney," Regina said in a honeyed tone, speaking directly to Charlotte. "We're both so looking forward to you vacationing with us up at Fowler's Folly."

Not a word about begging Charlotte to go there to shut down some sort of drug distribution network that was endangering the Fowlers—not that Charlotte, faced with her embarrassed and sweating former husband, had a thought to spare for anything other than what the hell Sydney was doing there—and as Regina's husband.

"Where's Gloria?" she asked, looking directly at Sydney and trying to remain calm. "Last I knew *Gloria* was your wife."

"That didn't work out," Sydney mumbled. "She went back to her family in New Jersey."

"*The* Family, don't you mean? Have you squared the casino scam with the government?" When he'd come to her to hide from his wife's relatives, Charlotte had made sure that Brenda had gotten her investment money back.

Sydney just shrugged and gave a little grin. It was maddening to Charlotte that that had always been Sydney's response to being in trouble—and doubly maddening that he usually got away with it.

Having struck and successfully thrown Charlotte off kilter, Regina smiled sweetly, pulled Sydney away, and did a royal wave to the surrounding tables on the way to hers.

41

The Diamonds and Brenda, by mutual consent, left the dinner early and, also by mutual consent, found a bar that was open. After a couple of drinks, they all were able to laugh about the Sydney sighting, even if a bit bitterly. Charlotte managed to lift a toast to Gloria for having escaped Sydney as Charlotte herself had.

When they'd reached the B&B, Charlotte, who had said nothing during the drive, said, "I think I'll take the boys for a walk."

"Would you like me to come along?" Brenda asked.

"No, I don't think so. When I come to bed I want my mind clear of this. A walk in the dark down a country lane with Sam and Rocket will put me back into a civilized mood, I think."

It was Sam who sensed the danger of the large, black sedan approaching from the rear at a fast pace but with its lights off. First Sam and then Rocket barked and, together, the dogs pulled to the right on their leashes, making Charlotte stumble off into the brush beside the road as the sedan roared past so close that its wheels almost went off onto the shoulder when it reached where Charlotte had been a split second earlier.

"Damn drunk drivers," Charlotte said, as she came up off her knees and surveyed the damage to her pants suit. "Thanks, guys," she said, lovingly patting each of her dogs in turn. "You're the best."

If her mind hadn't been preoccupied with the shock of Sydney Morrison's appearance—and, no less, that he now was married to Regina Fowler and Charlotte had to be in the same house with them for the next week—she might have given a thought to whether that really had been just a drunk driver.

She really should have given what happened more thought.

Chapter Three: Fowler's Folly

"Are you OK, Charlotte?" Marilyn asked as she sat down at the table set for four in the dining room of the Magnolia Bed and Breakfast the next morning. Charlotte and Brenda were already there, Brenda putting her fork down with her omelet having been partly eaten and picking up her coffee cup, while Charlotte polished off her own omelet and looked speculatively over at what Brenda hadn't finished. "Chance will be down in a few minutes. I still can't get over what a shock it must have been for you to see Sydney at the dinner last night."

"Like a plug nickel, he always plunks down at the most surprising times," Charlotte answered sourly. "I won't repeat it anywhere else—and will deny I ever said it—but I can't think of a better curse to happen to Regina Fowler than a marriage to Sydney."

"A plug nickel? Shouldn't that be a bad penny?"

"Even a bad penny is worth more than a plug nickel," Charlotte said, "unless someone like Regina is fool enough to pick it up and pass it off to the next unexpecting woman."

Brenda threw her head back and let loose with one of her signature laughs—this led to the other guests at other tables looking up startled, clearly recognizing the laugh from the movies. Only then did they seem to notice the movie star in their midst and begin to whisper not so surreptitiously among themselves.

Charlotte reacted by staring back at them, which caused the other diners to return their attention to their own breakfasts, without stopping hushed discussion across the tables. Charlotte's perusal of the room caused her to note who wasn't there. Well, who wasn't there other than Chance, as yet. His place was set up at their table in anticipation of his arrival. But there were no other unused place settings that Charlotte could see in the dining room other than an empty table on the other side of the room in a bow window.

Colonel Forest was just then moving through the room with a coffee pot and had come close to Charlotte's table. She extended an arm and arrested his movement with a hand on his sleeve. He looked at her expectantly, although more of his attention was going to refilling Brenda's coffee cup. Brenda gave him a dazzling smile, and the man almost melted on the spot.

"I don't see Samantha Fowler in here this morning," Charlotte said to the host. "I had wanted to talk to her this morning. Has she not come down yet?"

"She left last night—an hour or so after returning from the dinner—not long after your party returned," the colonel answered. "I expected she would be staying the night, but she didn't. She said there was some business she had to attend to. I was just turning off one of the TVs when she came in—a report was running on the hurricane approaching the coast. That seemed to upset Ms. Fowler. She said she had to get home. I guess if the storm goes over the Blue Ridge, Fowler's Folly might be in danger. It's right on the crest."

"Yes, I certainly hope the hurricane doesn't veer in that direction," Brenda said.

Colonel Forest looked perplexed.

"That's where we're headed today too," Marilyn explained.

"Ah, well, then good luck to you. Ms. Fowler said nothing yesterday about your being her house guests." One of the other diners caught his eye and he was off with the coffee pot.

"What was it you wanted to talk with Samantha about, Charlotte?" Marilyn asked after Colonel Forest had moved off. "As I recall you weren't any more enthused over Samantha than you were over Regina when we were at school. You certainly didn't go out of your way to be there whenever she came down to Elon to check up on Regina."

"In keeping with what the colonel said just now," Charlotte answered, "I wanted to check on whether Samantha knew we'd been invited up to Fowler's Folly. It would be just like Regina to fail to mention that to her older sister. Samantha certainly made no effort to talk to us last night."

"Our leaving as soon as the food service ended probably accounted for that," Chance said, arriving at last at the table.

"Probably right," Marilyn said, with a chuckle. "Samantha looked like she was soliciting the whole room for bailout funds for the college. I'm sure she would have gotten around to us soon, if we'd stayed."

Charlotte stood from the table.

"You don't have to clear out just because I've arrived," Chance said.

"Not a bit of it," Charlotte said, her eyes looking lovingly at Brenda's half-eaten omelet. "I still have some packing to do. I'd best do that—and retrieve Sam and Rocket and walk them before we start up into the mountains."

It was while she was walking the dogs along the road between the B&B and the town that she noticed the skid marks and remembered them from the near miss of the night before. She hadn't given that encounter any thought before, as Brenda had still been awake and in the mood to talk—and other things—when Charlotte got into bed.

Charlotte took a good look now, though. She could see where she had gone into the bushes off to the side of the road. And now, looking at the scene in the daylight, it looked like the car had made every effort to pull all the way over to the side of the road at that point. Somehow last night Charlotte hadn't felt that the car had come that close to hitting her—nor had the whole setup looked as intentional as it did in the light of day.

* * * *

"Sorry, I'm late in getting packed," Brenda said. "But Charlotte's not back with the dogs yet."

"No hurry, I'm afraid," Chance said, standing at the door to Brenda and Charlotte's B&B room. "We're not going anywhere for a while."

"Why not? What are those?"

"These are pieces of the radiator hose from the car's engine," Chance said. "Obviously purposely cut."

"I don't know how that could have happened. I'll call someone right away. Do you have AAA? Never mind if you don't." Colonel Forester said. He had arrived and was fluttering around Chance, clearly concerned.

"What's the matter? Marilyn is down at the entrance, so mad about something that she can't speak." Charlotte and the boys had arrived.

"Someone sabotaged the car," Chance said, showing Charlotte the cut hose. "Someone wants to make this a memorable vacation for us—or perhaps just stop our vacation before it begins."

"Probably just random vandalism," Brenda said. "Has anyone checked the other cars in the lot?"

"Oh, my God, I hadn't thought about that," the colonel said. "I'll call the garage on your car and then go check the other cars. But, believe me, this has never happened here before. We don't really have vandalism like this in Elon."

"Until now," Charlotte said. But the colonel was already gone.

"I'm packed now," Brenda said.

"I don't think Marilyn has finished," Chance said. "I'll go calm her down and see that we're ready for when the car is ready. I assume we go on with our plans."

Both Chance and Charlotte looked at Brenda. "Certainly," Brenda said. "It was just a bit of vandalism. The whole town is probably on edge over the threat of the college closing. Charlotte and the dogs and I can go down to the patio to sit and wait for the repairs to be done. Maybe the colonel will stand us for another cup of coffee."

"I'm sure the colonel will give you anything you want, Brenda," Charlotte said, with a smirk.

As soon as they settled on the patio, Charlotte pulled out her cell phone. "I guess I should give Regina a call. I'd still like to make sure we're welcome up at Fowler's Folly." She checked a slip of paper in her purse, keyed in the number, and waited for an answer.

When it came, she scowled, put her hand over the phone, and muttered an, "Oh, shit."

"What is it?" Brenda asked, looking concerned. But Charlotte raised a hand to cut her off.

"Sydney? This is Charlotte. I was calling Regina." She paused to listen to a babble that Brenda could hear from where she was sitting. Then she resumed. "What I wanted to know was whether we're really welcome up there—expected." A pause and then, "OK, good, but it probably will be late afternoon before we get up there. We're having a bit of car trouble."

When she rung off, Brenda said, "I take it Regina wasn't available and you got Sydney."

"Yes."

"On Regina's cell phone."

"Yes, apparently so."

"Well, I think that went well. You remained quite calm. So, he says we still should come up."

"Yes, he says we're expected. He said Regina wasn't available at the moment. He sounded funny, though. I know Sydney and his voices. He's up to something. I just don't know what it is. I hope to hell it isn't the drug distribution business. He's gotten himself into some serious trouble with the law before, but nothing that heavy. I'd hate to have to arrest him, not that I have that power anymore."

"I would think that you'd delight in it—putting Sydney in handcuffs," Brenda said. She started to laugh, but, when she caught the expression on Charlotte's face, she stopped.

"I don't want to have anything to do with the bastard," Charlotte said. "If I arrested him, I'll be tied up in his prosecution. I just want him out of my life—again."

They sat and drank coffee for several minutes. They could hear the arrival of the tow truck around at the front of the house, which was a good sign. Sam and Rocket were enjoying the time alone with their mistresses, exchanging places to receive pats and strokes.

"I know you want to see the house," Charlotte said. "If it weren't for that, I'd be in favor of switching our vacation to Asheville again and calling Evan and telling him someone else would need to go up there. I've had enough of the Fowler crew and we're not even there yet."

"I know you, Charlotte Diamond," Brenda said. "This case—with those green palm tree logos on the packets of drugs—is your case. I know you see it that way, and I understand. I know you really won't let contact with Sydney and Regina stand in your way of checking out

48

Fowler's Folly. But while we're on the subject of what I want to see, I have a confession to make. I'm glad it's just you here at the moment."

"A confession?"

"Yes, it took a while for me to realize it, but I've been to Fowler's Folly before—although I think the family was still referring to it as Fowler's Retreat at the time—trying to stave off the other name taking hold. And I didn't connect the name 'Fowler' as I should."

"You've been there? How did that occur?"

"You know the head of the spiritualist colony Chance spoke of—Samantha Fowler's brother. Not her father, who started it—her brother who took it over and built it up?"

"You went on a spiritualist retreat?"

"No. Worse than that," Brenda said. "Samantha's brother. His name was Frederick. Frederick Fowler."

"Yes, that name sounds familiar. And so?"

"And so, I was there for visits a couple of times—at Fowler's Folly—in the mid seventies. I was there because I was married to Frederick Fowler once for two days. But he was more familiar to me by his movie name—Frederick Fulton. I didn't know until we got the license what his legal surname was."

* * * *

The first leg of the drive up to Fowler's Folly, on Piney Mountain, near the Wintergreen resort, in Virginia's Nelson County, was a tense one inside Chance Diamond's repaired Avalon. Chance and Marilyn caught the icy vibes coming from Charlotte in the backseat, followed by the uncharacteristic quiet of the usually effervescent Brenda, but they said nothing. They'd experienced such periods in their own marriage, and, although they hadn't observed one in the young marriage between Charlotte and Brenda yet,

49

they were realistic enough to know that minor disagreements and pouts were inevitable even in a same-sex marriage.

The root of the problem was that immediately after Brenda had dropped the bombshell on Charlotte that she'd been married to Frederick Fowler, Chance had appeared to let them know the Avalon was fixed and it was time to shove off.

It wasn't until they stopped for lunch in the Rockfish Valley, in the folds of the mountains on the eastern slopes of the Blue Ridge Mountains, that there was an opportunity to relieve the pressure. They stopped at a brewery that served food, the Devil's Backbone, on the turnoff from Highway 151 to go up into the mountains. After watering and feeding Sam and Rocket, they took a table on the patio to be able to keep the dogs with them and had a very quiet lunch.

At the end of the meal, Charlotte stood and said, "I'll take the dogs on a relief walk over in that meadow. Perhaps you'll come with me, Brenda." It sounded more like a command than a request to the other three.

Chance didn't catch on quick enough and said, "I'll be happy to take the dogs. I think it's my turn."

Marilyn, though, placed a hand on his arm to keep him from rising, and said, pointedly, "I think Charlotte and Brenda want to do it, honey." He sank back into his chair, finally "getting it."

"You were married to Frederick Fowler?" Charlotte said when they were well away from the restaurant.

"Yes, for two days, very early in my film career."

"And you slept with him?"

"Of course. That's not unusual even for those married for only a couple of days. After Tony's father, I was determined not to sleep with a man without a wedding ring. So, I married him. Both you and I had a full life before we met, Charlotte, which included sleeping with men. You

50

slept with Evan Worthington and, of course, with Sydney, didn't you?"

"Yes, of course. It just came as a shock to hear, Brenda. I didn't know. You didn't . . ."

"It was disclosed when we got a marriage license," Brenda said. "Even his name. I guess you didn't zero in on that at the time because you were as head over heels as I was."

"OK, granted. All I could think about was that you actually were marrying me. But Frederick Fowler . . . how . . . why?"

"That was the first time I wanted David Runyon to make love to me and he rebuffed me." David Runyon, who Brenda only learned years later was gay, was her leading man in many of her films. And throughout that time, Brenda had a crush on him and had done her best to land him, not knowing that he preferred men. "I got drunk and went to Las Vegas with Freddie and wound up married to him as some sort of misguided 'take that, David Runyon' gesture."

"But it's such a coincidence. How did you even know Fowler?"

"He was an actor in my early film days. Fredrick Fulton. He was in the movie we'd just finished—I don't remember its title—and he was trying to romance me while I was unsuccessfully and frustratingly trying to entice David. Freddie was handsome and had incredible charisma. I can well believe he could become the guru in a spiritualist colony. He knew how to project sincerity, and he could get what he wanted with just a smile. I was wounded and bruised. He said we really should be celebrating in Las Vegas—we were in Los Angeles at the time. I said I'd never been there. He had a snazzy yellow Ford convertible—just like the one I'd seen in the movie *Giant*—and he said we could be in Las Vegas in a jiffy.

"We partied there and he propositioned me. I said I'd sleep with no man but my husband. He said that could easily be remedied—there were wedding chapels on every corner in Las Vegas and no waiting time. I was in the mood to punish David. Every man in Hollywood wanted to sleep with me other than the man I wanted. I, of course, had no idea that, although he was affectionate to me, there could be no romantic spark there for David. So, I married Frederick and spent the night with him. I sobered up the next morning, contacted the studio, and although the publicity department gleefully had a field day over it all, the producer of the film we'd just put into the can, Aaron Woolridge, guided me through a quickie divorce. And that was that—except for the boost we got in publicity for the movie."

"OK, I can see all of that," Charlotte said. "Sorry I got bent out of shape on it. But you said you'd been to Fowler's Folly."

"Yes, a couple of times, for the weekend. Several in the movie cast did. I remember now that it was a Civil War movie. We filmed for a month near Richmond. Freddie invited us up to his family home. The place was spooky and out of place in the mountains, but the house was quite a palace. A little run down, though."

"So, did you meet any of the cousins we'll be seeing?"

"Just Samantha, Freddie's sister. I'd forgotten her name. She wasn't at all impressed by the influx of movie folks. Me, in particular. She must have sensed that Freddie was interested in me. She was stiff and borderline hostile. That was one of the first things I thought about when I woke with Freddie in my bed in Las Vegas—that I was now Samantha's sister-in-law."

"I can see where that gave you the creeps."

"You bet," Brenda said, her signature tinkling laugh back now that the tension was drained from the atmosphere. "I immediately thought of the movie *Giant* then too—part of which was filmed near where we are now. The character of Rock Hudson married Elizabeth Taylor's character in Virginia and took her home to his ranch in Texas—and to his resentful and sour sister, played by Mercedes McCambridge. It couldn't be more apt to a trip up to Fowler's Folly—even now. But in some ways I'm looking forward to it."

When they had returned to the restaurant, the women went in to use the restroom and Chance took the dogs to the car. As they left the restaurant, Marilyn whispered to Brenda—Charlotte had walked ahead at a faster pace, being taller and having longer legs than the other two as well as being the more impatient of the trio— "Everything fine now? I sense something has been relieved."

"Yes, we're all good now," Charlotte turned her head and answered for the two of them. "I'll leave it for Brenda to tell you about it later. I'm sure you'll be as floored by what she says as I was. We might consider this to be a form of that hurricane that always hits when I vacation on the East Coast."

* * * *

Charlotte stewed as the Avalon started climbing the foothills on a two-lane, winding road that would pass the entrance to the Wintergreen resort on the right and the more hidden one up to the top of Piney Mountain on the left before cresting at the top of the Blue Ridge and intersecting the Blue Ridge Parkway. The parkway was the longer, southern stretch of roadway running north to south along the top of the Blue Ridge Mountains, one of the oldest mountain chains in the world. This road provided one of the few "across the mountains" intersections with the parkway between Roanoke and where it started at the end of the Skyline Drive between Charlottesville, in the east, and Waynesboro, in the west.

Charlotte had a lot to think about. She was riding into the jaws of irritation from Regina Fowler and her own former husband, Sydney. She knew now that Brenda was riding into a similar situation with Samantha Fowler, who briefly had been her sister-in-law. She had also been asked by Regina—and then the FBI—to find out if there was a connection between Fowler's Folly and a drug distribution operation coming up from South America.

The president of Elon College had also asked Charlotte to check on whether either Samantha or Regina had been involved in millions of missing dollars from the college endowment fund. And the supposed near automobile accident the previous night when she was walking the dogs couldn't float out of her mind.

It was quite a burden of thought. But it didn't stop her from noticing when Chance had made a left on the even steeper and narrower, more winding road up to the top of Piney Mountain, that the roadway was being widened toward the hillside. The road was quite narrow as it existed, barely allowing two sedans to pass side by side. But land was being cleared and leveled to make the road wider. Quite an expensive proposition she thought, and an obvious indication that the access to Fowler's Folly was being improved. Also an indication that this improvement was requiring a significant outlay of money.

There also was evidence, as the impressive Italianate palace came into view, that renovations were under way there too. The front of the building had been cleaned and the huge marble stones making up the walls had been repointed. The eastern side of the castle was covered with scaffolding, indicating that the entire façade was being refurbished. In contrast, the smaller version of the palace that they passed before coming into the turning circle of the larger building's entrance, was in an advanced stage of ruin, the second story seemingly having sunk into the ground floor. The ravages of a fire were evident, but the growth of thick vines over the structure indicated the worst damage had been done decades later.

"Isn't that a shame?" Marilyn said as they drove past the ruins. "They seem to be letting the smaller version of the mansion just collapse."

"I don't know, I think it's beautiful in its own way," Brenda said. "Both sad and romantic at the same time. Very much the English folly, all the more poignant because it wasn't intentionally built to be a folly. Both desolate and deserted."

"Not deserted, I don't think," Marilyn countered. "I think I just saw movement there at the side. Right over . . . maybe not. If it ever was there, it's gone now. Do you suppose we're already seeing evidence of haunting?"

"Are Methodist ministers supposed to believe in ghosts?" Brenda asked, with a laugh.

"Methodist ministers can have fun with the concept, just like anyone else," Marilyn responded with a laugh of her own. "What do you think of it, Charlotte?"

"Think of what? Oh, the ruins of the smaller house. It's pretty far gone is what I think."

"You sound like you're pretty far gone too," Brenda said, with another laugh. "You are far away. Mesmerized by the bigger house?"

"Yes, I suppose so," Charlotte said. But it wasn't really that that had gotten her attention. It was two other sightings. First was what she saw off in the distance, where the meadow the house sat in merged into a dense forest of trees. Right there at the edge of the clearing stood a stocky man, legs set in a wide stance, dressed out in English hunting togs, and with a rifle held loosely in the crook of his arm. As far as Charlotte knew, it wasn't hunting season in Virginia. It certainly wasn't in Maryland. Could it be security for the property? He certainly didn't look fit or young enough to be a professional watchman. And he was dressed more for an English country weekend movie set than for the mountains of Virginia. Brenda would be pleased at that thought, Charlotte knew, but for some reason she didn't want to draw her spouse's attention to the hunter.

She similarly didn't want to draw her attention to the second, unsettling sight she was looking at. There were cars pulled up in a line on the trampled and brown grass off the turning circle below the entrance stairs to the big house. The sporty red Lexus coup begged for attention, and the practical white Forester with a logo on the side was an expected farm vehicle for an estate this size. But Charlotte's gaze was captured by the other two vehicles. They were identical, both huge, sedate, black sedans. Neither looked like an American style. The sighting of the hunter had put "English" into Charlotte's mind. This isn't what bothered her, though. Now that she thought about it and set the image of the cars in her mind, this was exactly the kind of car that had almost run her down the previous night on the road by the Elon B&B.

As they drew up to the entrance, the main door—double and of heavy wood—opened and three figures appeared: a tall, gaunt man in a black suit, the butler or a mortician, Charlotte thought; a young, blonde woman in a simple frock that made her look like the ingénue in one of Brenda's movies; and . . . unfortunately . . . the all-too-familiar Sydney Morrison—or Sydney Fowler now, as, to add to Charlotte's irritation, Regina had told her at the banquet the night before that Sydney had changed his name to conform with the Fowler family's expectations of loyalty and homage of even in-laws.

As the four of them disembarked from the Avalon, neither the young woman nor the presumed butler showing any signs of coming out to help them with their luggage, Sydney did skip down the steps and move toward them.

But Charlotte quickly figured out that he had no intention of carrying bags either. He went straight for Charlotte and drew her off to the side.

"I must talk to you about something, Charlotte. I need your help."

"I think you're beyond my help," Charlotte said somewhat icily.

"You're police. You can't help not helping with something like this," he said and then rushed on. "It's Regina. She's missing."

"Missing?"

"Yes. We drove back separately last night—the three of us. I was the last one to arrive. I stopped at a bar before coming up the mountain."

"Naturally," Charlotte interjected acidly.

He ignored her and went on. "When I got here, Regina and Samantha were having a deathly row in the master's study. I avoided them and went straight to our room. Regina never arrived there. When I asked Samantha about it this morning, she just said she didn't know—or care—where Regina is. Charlotte, those two have been at each other's throats for two weeks over this property deal."

"What property deal?" Charlotte asked.

But at that moment the gaunt figure in the black suit came alive and called out, "This way, folks." Which Charlotte thought was quite obvious. It certainly was the front door and it certainly was open.

He made no move to come down the stairs and help with the luggage. Chance had the bulk of it, and Marilyn was carrying her overnight bag. Charlotte muttered to Sydney a sotto voce, "How long have you been married to Regina, Sydney?"

"Uh, six months."

"Not nearly long enough for you to have figured Regina out. She's just doing her theatrics. If she hasn't come out of the woodwork in a couple of hours to needle

57

and gloat, I'll see what we can do. We can talk about this later, when we're checked into this pile of marble." She shoved Brenda's suitcase in his hand, hefted her own, with her overnight bag in the other hand, and marched up the steps.

"I'm Curtis, the butler," the gaunt man said as he stood back for Chance and Charlotte to struggle through the door, followed, in more stately form, by Marilyn and Brenda, chattering happily to each other. Sam and Rocket followed on leashes held by Marilyn.

"I'm Janice, the general dogs body around here," the young woman said in a soft voice with a nice smile. "Come in, please, and welcome to Fowler's Retreat."

"Fowler's Retreat?" Charlotte asked.

"We're trying to change the image of the place," Janice said.

"And the state of repair too," Charlotte said. "It must be costing a bundle. Who's paying for all of this—and the widening of the road?"

"Yes, updating as well," the young woman answered in a somewhat flustered tone.

Charlotte noticed that she didn't say where the money was coming from to do this renovation—not to mention what Sydney alluded to in the way of a property deal—but she'd pursue that later. For now, she looked around the large, columned foyer with the Carrara marble columns and floor tiles in a rich tan color with black veining. The look extended into the two large reception rooms on either side of the foyer. And behind one of the columns for just the briefest of moments, she spied a flurry of cobalt-blue silk robes; a pretty, but aging and heavily painted face; and a blood-red turban. The apparition was there for no more than a second.

Clea Fowler, Charlotte thought—the younger cousin. She didn't have time to speculate further, though, as at the sound of rustling from beyond the curve of the grand staircase straight ahead, she looked up to the two-story landing and at the dazzling portrait in stained glass of a standing woman in a full-length scarlet velvet ball gown, with a plunging neckline.

Claudia Fowler, the first wife of Franklin Fowler, the builder of Fowler's Folly. Neither Charlotte nor the other women in her party needed to be told who was depicted in the light-backed stained glass. Whether lit directly from the sun or from an artificial source, the effect of the artwork was startling and jaw dropping. It was a genuine Tiffany design; cost, even when it was originally commissioned, more than the fortunes of the richest hundred in American; and was featured from time to time in magazines and museum art books. Chance had shown them an image of it on his laptop the previous evening.

The gasps from the three women were intensified, though, when the source of the rustling—a tall woman, with straight back, and garbed in the very dress depicted in the stained-glass window—rounded the curve in the staircase to stand on the landing, below the window, and effecting the exact same pose as the woman in the window.

Samantha Fowler, Claudia's granddaughter, and the spitting image of her.

Everyone held their breath for a dramatic moment, but it was Samantha herself who broke the spell.

"You brought dogs." The voice was accusatory.

"Regina included them in the invitation," Charlotte, unimpressed and unbowed, shot back.

"Of course she did," Samantha said, her voice sour and condescending.

Chapter Four: Lay of the Land

"Oh, there you are. Your room is down the hall, Brenda."

"No, it isn't. This one will be fine for us," Charlotte said, giving Samantha a level look. "We don't need two rooms. Perhaps Regina didn't tell you. Brenda and I are married. So, we only need the one room. This one is very nice, thank you."

Charlotte almost laughed when Samantha arrived in the guest bedroom corridor not more than fifteen minutes after her grand entrance down the staircase in the foyer in her red-velvet gown, obviously meant to impress them—which, Charlotte reluctantly admitted, it did. Now Samantha was dressed in brown and green suede, complete with brown leather gloves. A regular Robin Hood. Charlotte wondered if it was the time of day that Samantha went out to survey her empire.

And the room, indeed, was quite nice—other than, perhaps, the smell of fresh paint. It also had its own well-appointed bathroom. Charlotte wondered if all of the rooms on this hall—there had to be at least ten of them—had their own baths. If so, it wouldn't take much to make Fowler's Folly a luxury boutique hotel. This wing was three stories tall, so maybe there were thirty rooms on this wing alone.

She'd been confused by the contrast as they were ushered by Janice to the second floor and down this hallway. In many ways, it appeared that the place was being renovated. In others—a hole in the wall here, a pulled-up floorboard there—it looked like preliminary demolition was under way. Janice had seen Charlotte assessing the conditions and, correctly assuming the questions in Charlotte's mind had said, "Some of the wiring has to be replaced in the renovations we're doing."

We? Charlotte had wondered. Just where did Janice fit into this household? Then again, as if she could read Charlotte's mind, Janice had said, "There is a larger staff here than just Curtis and me. We are the front contingent. He supervises and I serve as Ms. Samantha's secretary and Ms. Clea's nurse. But there are cooks and maids behind the scenes. It takes quite a few people to try to keep up with this house."

"I'll bet," Charlotte had said. "You don't have duties dedicated to Regina?"

"No," Janice had said, with a tight-lipped look, leaving her response at just the one terse word.

And now Samantha had come to check on them, while Janice took Chance and Marilyn farther down the hall to their room. Curtis had made a gesture in the foyer to take Sam and Rocket away, but Charlotte had balked and had been accommodated. The two pooches would room with her and Brenda.

"No, Regina didn't tell me that you two were married," Samantha said. "Congratulations." The sentiment didn't make it into Samantha's eyes. "Perhaps you can spare Brenda for a time when you're unpacked. There's something I'd like to show her."

"Yes, of course, I can suspend this now, if you wish," Brenda answered.

"That would be satisfactory," Samantha said. "If you have sensible shoes for the outdoors, they would be appropriate. What I want to show you is a distance across the lawns."

"Will these do?" Brenda asked, taking a pair of worn sneakers from her suitcase.

"Yes, certainly," Samantha answered regally, showing every sign of trying to convey that such scuffed sneakers weren't really appropriate wear for anywhere on the grounds. Brenda didn't take offense. She just smiled, no doubt knowing that that would deflate Samantha more than being regal in turn. The whole world knew of Brenda's serene dignity. Samantha's, not so much.

"You go on ahead," Charlotte said to Brenda. "I'll finish unpacking for both of us." She hoped that would be a message to Samantha on how closely she and Brenda were married, and from the sour look Samantha gave, the message had shot home.

As the two women departed the room, Sydney, who must have been lurking in the hall the whole time, slithered into it. Both Sam and Rocket came up on their haunches and bared their teeth. Charlotte motioned to them that everything was OK, and they went back into a crouch, but neither took their eyes off Sydney and both looked like they'd pounce and chew him up at the slightest provocation.

The dogs had come into Charlotte and Brenda's life post Sydney, but that hadn't hindered them instinctively knowing he wasn't a friend. Charlotte marked in her mind that the two dogs, neither of which had had the occasion to know Sydney, were a much better judge of his character—or lack of it—than she had been.

"Could we talk about Regina now?" Sydney asked when he was sure Samantha and Brenda were far enough down the hall that they wouldn't hear and that he wasn't destined to be the dogs' afternoon snack.

"I suppose so," Charlotte answered. "But there are some other explanations I would like to have from you as well."

"Such as?" Charlotte could see Sydney steeling himself for the inevitable questions, but she didn't start with what she knew he was expecting.

"For starters, who belongs to what car out in the parking circle?"

Sydney gave her a look of surprise. "What does that—?"

"Just answer the questions, Sydney."

He shrugged. "The Lexus coup is mine . . . and, no, I didn't steal it. The Bentley's belong to the estate. Samantha and Regina drive them. Clea doesn't drive. Her husband, Rupert . . ."

"Excuse me. Rupert?"

"You haven't met him yet. He's from England. Claims to be a Sir something, but I have my doubts."

"Pudgy and florid, given to hunting clothes and rifles?"

"Yes, that's him."

"I've seen him at a distance. Proceed."

"He drives a Land Rover, but it's in the shop. It always seems to be in the shop. And the Forester is an estate car, driven usually by Curtis or Janice. The rest of the staff parks behind by the service entrances. But why do you ask?"

As if he hadn't asked the question, Charlotte continued. "Who drove the Bentleys, which I take it are those big, black globs of metal out there, last night?"

"We all drove up from the college banquet separately—Regina and Samantha in the Bentleys and me in the Lexus. We had gone to Elon separately. I came from meetings in Richmond. Both of the Bentleys were here when I arrived last night. So were the Land Rover and

Forester. Curtis and Rupert took the Land Rover down to Lynchburg this morning."

"Why were you in Richmond? What sort of scam do you have going now?"

Sydney gave her a wounded look. "No scam. A consortium of investors want to buy this place and turn it into a boutique hotel with a golf course. Great location—when it's easier to get to it. Gorgeous views. This house is practically set up like a hotel already. It was a retreat center once."

"And what con do you have going with this scheme? How many slices over a full pie are you trying to cut this deal into?"

"Charlotte, you wound me."

"You can bet I've had numerous reasons to. Of all the nonsense I won't forgive you for, scamming Brenda by selling her shares in your casino scheme ranks at the top. What is all of this—this renovation and the resort plans—to you?"

"I've been putting the deal together for over a year. Imagining the concept, finding the investors, finding out what has to be done before they'd buy into it."

"That's what the renovations and the widening of the road up to here are about?"

"Yes," Sydney answered. "There's already a landing strip finished too. Samantha insisted on having that in early. We're trying to make the property as attractive to the wealthy as possible. I'm arranging all that. The family brought me in—the Fowler cousins. That's what I was doing when Regina and I decided to marry."

"And whose idea was that?"

"Whose idea was what?"

"The idea of getting married. Yours? Regina's?"

"Regina's, I guess," he said, looking somewhat sheepish. And then, evidently trying to deflect the direction of the discussion, "You know Regina has always had a soft spot for you, Charlotte."

"I think both of you have soft spots, but if you comb your hair right . . . so, who's putting up the front money for the renovations?"

"I don't know. The Fowlers just seem to have the money when I need it to do the work. Although there's more work than I bargained for."

"The vandalism part?"

Sydney looked at her in surprise. "How did you know we were being vandalized?"

"Janice told me that the little acts of destruction here and there were caused by rewiring, which I don't believe for a moment. Are you finding opposition to this resort deal?"

"Maybe," Sydney answered. "But it could be the legend too—there's supposed to be a stash of money hidden somewhere here. Regina says they've always had problems with fortune hunters stealing in and trying to find it. Causes a lot of damage, though. You can bet I'm not telling the investors' group about that. I've thought of salting something somewhere and 'discovering' it so we can put that to rest. But I haven't found money to do that."

"Someone's pouring money into this," Charlotte muttered. "So, my next to last question—"

"Next to last?"

"Yes, you know what my last question is." She went on as Sydney shuddered noticeably. "What were Samantha and Regina fighting about last night? I know you. I know you came close enough to hear what they were shouting. Was it about this land deal, or was it about my coming up here? You should know that Regina asked me to come. Something about drugs—connected with a case I've worked before. But it's obvious Samantha doesn't want us here."

"I don't know anything about drugs," Sydney said defensively. "You know I've never been into the drug scene."

"I'm not sure I know half of what you've been up to. The fight?"

"Some of both, I guess. Samantha hit the roof when Regina told her she'd asked you to come up—not just you. Regina said who else would be in your party. I thought Samantha was going to go bananas about the dogs, but it was Brenda Boynton that sent her over the edge. I don't know what that was about, though."

"I think I do. What else did they fight about? Does Samantha not want to sell Fowler's Folly?"

"It's not that, exactly. They both want to get out from underneath this place, but—"

"Both? There are three of them. What about Clea?"

"No one consults with Clea on such things. She's off in her own little world. I suspect that Rupert cares, but Samantha and Regina do what they can to freeze him out of any information. I have to know a lot to get the deal done and the property prepared for it, but I don't think they tell me any more than I absolutely have to know either. No, the argument was over the timing. Regina wants to sell as soon as possible, and Samantha wants to sell but not before the end of the year. And when those two can't agree on anything, the atmosphere around here is toxic. I'm really scared about Regina, Charlotte. It's not like her not to be here to try to top Samantha's grand entrances when we have visitors. I'm afraid that something serious might have happened last night. Samantha can get quite violent. And there's no familial lovey-doveyness between any of the three of them."

"OK, no other cars up here, you say?"

"Only the kitchen and maid staff's personal cars, and none of them claimed one of their vehicles was missing."

"So, she's still up here unless she walked down the mountain, which isn't likely. That means the two of us will have to do some looking. You start—or continue, if you've already been looking. I'll get to it after I've unpacked."

Sydney thanked her and started to back his way out the door. He wasn't about to turn his back on Sam and Rocket.

"Not so fast. The last question, which you knew was coming. If you're legally married to Regina—and for all I know, you are now—what happened to Gloria?"

"She's back in New Jersey. Her people didn't take a liking to me, and we thought it best if we split up. Still like her, though, and she's working this investor consortium angle too."

"Christ, Sydney, you tried to screw her relatives over the casino hotel deal, knowing they were Mafia? And you're trying to bring the New Jersey Mafia into this resort deal? Do you have a death wish, or something?"

"There's good money to be made in this," he said, using his "I'm hurt" voice.

"You want a mausoleum, not just a gravestone? God, you're the limit, Sydney. Just go before I start pulling my hair out and rending my garments. And speaking of garments, bring me a scarf or something that's Regina's and I'll put the puppies on search duty."

Sam and Rocket took the tone of her voice as an invitation to bare their teeth and growl, which they did— and which caused Sydney to back to the door. Charlotte also made her zaftig body rise to full height and breadth.

Eyes wide open, Sydney murmured "cadaver dogs?" in a hollow voice.

"Oh, good grief, Sydney. Dogs can follow the scent of live people as well as dead. You're the one who's hinting Regina might be dead. My vote is that she's just preparing for a dramatic entrance when we least expect and want it. That's one of her specialties."

Sydney's eyes narrowed again. "You never did like Regina, did you?"

"You knew before you married her that I didn't like Regina, Sydney. Hell, you knew it before you married me. Now shoo. Go. Boo. I'll get to searching when I'm done here."

To the tune in harmony of deep dog growls Sydney evaporated from the room.

* * * *

"How far away is this place you want to show me?" Brenda asked. They were already across the meadow surrounding the main house at the top of the mountain and had moved into the shade of the woods. Although there had been no evidence of it until they reached the edge of the woods, there was a path freshly lined with shredded tree bark taking a gently winding route into the dense foliage.

"Not far," Samantha said. She was stiff, abrupt in her language, and walking with a determined stride.

People usually melted to the charm of Brenda. Not so with Samantha.

"My, what's that ahead? It looks like a small graveyard."

"Yes, it's the Fowler family graveyard. That's what I want to show you."

They pulled up in front of a large, rose-granite tombstone. The cemetery was shaded and immaculately cared for. There must have been nearly twenty gravesites in it dominated by a central mausoleum, which captured Brenda's eye as they moved inside a six-foot iron fence, set there, no doubt, to keep the deer and other critters out. The names Franklin and Mae Fowler could clearly be seen carved above the door of the mausoleum, and, given identical death dates, Brenda was able to ascertain that Mae had been Franklin's last wife—the grandmother of Clea.

68

Having walked on and stopped in front of another tombstone, she redirected her eyes and then opened them wide.

"This is Freddie's tomb. Frederick Fowler," Brenda exclaimed. She automatically knelt in front of the stone and laid a hand on it. "I'd heard he died, but I didn't know where or when. He died of a self-inflicted gunshot wound, didn't he?"

"He was dead before he shot himself. Look at the inscription," Samantha said, with a hard-edged voice.

The inscription under the birth and death dates said, "Died of unrequited love."

"Unrequited love. What does that mean?" Brenda murmured.

"You should know. He died as most of the Fowler men have died. He shot himself—and in the usual place, the master's study at the house. That's what made his breathing stop. But he had died to the world before then. He died because of you."

"Because of me? I don't understand."

"I'm not surprised. You lured him and used him and then discarded him."

"I'm sorry, Samantha," Brenda said, looking up at the seething woman towering over her and suddenly feeling vulnerable. "I know Freddie was your brother, but I don't know what he told you of our brief—really brief—marriage. We were both young and drunk. I was rebounding from an unsatisfactory infatuation that was going nowhere. He was just randy. We were in a movie together that had just wrapped up. We were giddy and celebrating. Neither one of us had been in many movies before. He wanted me to see Las Vegas and drove me there. We married while three-quarters loaded and feeling on top of the world. We saw the mistake as soon as we woke up the next day, and then just as quickly undid what we'd done. Nobody would even have known, if the studio

69

hadn't thought it would be great PR for the film. I know we both immediately forgot about it. It was just the way Hollywood was in those days."

"You may have forgotten about it. Frederick never did. He was never the same after you lured him into bed and then discarded him."

"Look, Samantha. I didn't lure him into anything. He pressured me and I was drunk and naïve—and bruised. There was nothing else to it."

"It killed him. It literally killed him. I understand from recent news reports that you have a son you've kept hidden. Another actor. His name is Tony Trice."

"What are you implying, Samantha? Are you suggesting that my son is Freddie's son?"

"I've seen photographs of him. He's the spitting image of Frederick."

"Most handsome men, especially those playing leading roles in Hollywood, can be seen to have similar features—especially if that's what you want to see. I assure you that Tony is not Freddie's son."

"So you say. Or you have denied a son to Frederick while he was alive and to the rest of my family now. Why should I believe you?"

"You can believe me because I can show you a birth certificate that shows Tony was born before I knew Freddie—before I went to Hollywood."

"Dates have been given on his birth. It would work out."

"Good grief, Samantha. No one in Hollywood is as old as their official records show. It's the movie world way. Although it's really no business of yours, after we return to Maryland, I'll have a copy of the certificate sent to you."

"All something you can buy," Samantha said, with venom. "And now you desecrate Frederick's memory and love for you further by marrying again . . . marrying a . . .

another woman. Did you even bother to get a divorce from Frederick?"

"Of course I got a divorce from Freddie. This is all ludicrous, Samantha. I'm sorry you've been developing this illusion over the years, but I assure you that's what it was. Freddie was a womanizer—he slept with several other starlets before leaving Hollywood. He probably even married a few of them. I'm sorry, but—"

"I'll leave you here to try to make peace with my brother," Samantha spat out. "I'll not bring it up again while you're here, but I do wish to see your son face to face. When I see him in the flesh, I'll know. I'll know if he's my brother's son—if he's a Fowler."

"I don't think that will happen, Samantha. And it isn't because there is the remotest chance that Tony is related to you by blood. And, yes, please. I would like to be left here alone for a few minutes if you don't mind. I was never in love with your brother, but I was very fond of him. I do wish to mourn the loss of him. I can find my way back to the house. In fact, I would prefer to."

Without further words, Samantha turned and marched away. When she had disappeared into a curve of the path into the woods, Brenda turned her face to Frederick Fowler's tombstone again, laid a hand on it, and lowered her face in prayer.

The first shot pinged off the headstone, taking a corner of the granite above Frederick's name with it. Instinctively, Brenda flattened herself on the ground, and worked to scoot around to the other side of the slab of granite, in search of cover.

The second shot rang out before she made it around to better shelter.

Chapter Five: Clea's Initial Trances

Charlotte and the dogs were outside, Charlotte looking at newly dug flower beds on the western side of the house. Sam and Rocket were snuffling around, having taken a whiff of one of Regina's scarves, but they weren't showing interest in the house foundation, wanting to pull Charlotte away from there. The sound of a shot, though, redirected their attention as well as Charlotte's. Before the second one sounded, they were all racing for the woods, where the sound of the shots had come from. Charlotte, not a marathon runner even in her best year, freed the dogs to race on ahead of her. Her training clicking in, her eyes scanned the tree line of the forest from one end to the other.

She saw three things in quick succession: the hint of a figure lurking around the ruins of the replica house but quickly disappearing; Rupert Fowler stumbling out of the tree line at a good distance to the north, not far from the ruins of the smaller house; and Samantha striding out of the woods straight ahead of Charlotte, from the direction Charlotte judged the shots to have sounded. After scanning the field, Charlotte's eyes went back to lock on Rupert, who had a hunting rifle nestled in the crook of his arm and a brace of rabbits dangling from one of his hands.

She kept her eyes on the rifle, prepared to hit the turf if he raised it, but he didn't. Even from this distance he looked slightly bemused.

Sam and Rocket raced right on by Samantha and into the woods as the woman bore down on Charlotte.

"Where did those shots come from?" Charlotte called out as Samantha came close.

Samantha was looking cool. She swiveled her head to the north and inclined her head. "It looks like Rupert again has shot game that no one in the house will want to see on the table."

"Where's Brenda? She was with you. You wanted to show her something."

"I did show her something," Samantha said. "She's still back in the woods. She wanted to be alone at her husband's grave."

"Her husband?" Charlotte said, but then realizing what Samantha meant, she said, "Is that where your brother, Frederick is buried?"

Visibly deflated that Charlotte knew about Frederick, Samantha voiced an icy "Yes," and passed Charlotte by en route to the house.

By then others had come out of the house too, but they retreated to the front door as Rupert approached from across the fields.

"If you don't want to be shot entering the house, I suggest you give me that rifle," Charlotte called out. "Did you fire those two shots we just heard?"

"No, I have no idea where those came from," Rupert said, looking confused. "Who are you?"

Charlotte would have ignored him and just snatched the rifle from him and continued on toward the woods, but she spied Brenda emerging from the path there with Sam and Rocket at her side. She looked fine, although she was walking a bit slowly.

"I'm Charlotte Diamond," she said hurriedly, fidgeting there in place but wanting to get to Brenda. "I was invited here by Regina. Someone has been firing near the house, and you appear to be the only one around with a rifle. I'm retired FBI. I again suggest that you just give me that rifle before going into the house. The shots we heard have everyone on edge, and someone might confront you with a firearm of their own."

Rupert meekly turned the rifle over with a muttered, "I didn't fire those shots. Only a fool would fire shots this near to the house," and continued on to the service area of the house with his rabbits. He had an English accent that completed the effect of the clothes he was wearing.

"Are you OK? We heard shots," Charlotte said, as she moved toward the approaching Brenda, now under the protection of two dogs.

"I'm a bit wobbly," Brenda answered, the wobbliness clear in her voice. "The shots were fired in my direction. I had to take refuge behind a tombstone. I can't see why they would have purposely been fired at me."

"Samantha took you to Frederick Fowler's grave," Charlotte said. "Did she have a reason for doing so?"

"She blames me for his death. She suggested that I hadn't really divorced him, and, worse, thinks that Tony is Frederick's son."

"Well, she's as crazy as the rest the bunch. We'll pack up and get out of here."

"No, please," Brenda said, laying a hand on Charlotte's arm. "The worst of that from Samantha is over I think, and you have a job to do here. Did you have reason to think there were drugs stashed at this side of the house?"

"No, the dogs and I were looking for Regina. According to Sydney she hasn't been in evidence since last night although she came back to Fowler's Folly last night. He wants me to find her."

"All the more reason for us to stick it out here, then," Brenda said. "I'll be more careful. I'll go in and take a nap and you can resume with the search. Can you manage with just one of the boys, though? It would be a help to have one of the dogs with me."

"Certainly. Take Rocket. He's the most intimidating. And lock the bedroom door. I'll be in when I can."

When Brenda had moved on, Charlotte examined the hunting rifle. It had been fired recently, but there were those two rabbits Rupert had been carrying, both of which had bullet holes in them. And he did seem to be genuinely startled by the suggestion he'd fired those two shots. She wanted to check out the ruins of the replica house more closely, but there was something else she wanted to check first. She strode off toward the path Samantha and Brenda had emerged from. Sam, panting, but happy as he could be to have one of his mistresses all to himself, trotted along beside her.

When she emerged from the woods again, she saw that the sky was overcast and it had started to sprinkle. She paused long enough to put in a cell phone call to Margaret Chafin, the interim president of Elon College.

"Professor Chafin, this is Charlotte Diamond. I'm up at Fowler's Folly. How is the campaign to keep the school open going?"

"It's hopeful," Professor Chafin answered. "If we only could count on the entire endowment—"

"Regina Fowler hasn't contacted you today, has she?" Charlotte broke in.

"She hasn't?" she responded to the college president's answer. "Well, she seems to be missing. She should be up here but isn't. I'll pursue that, but there's something else you could have checked out for me, if you will. It's about the endowment issue."

75

When Charlotte rang off, the rain had picked up a bit. She'd have to put off her inspection of the replica house for now. She'd have to get into the main house if she didn't want to be soaked.

"Go on ahead, boy," she said to Sam, "find Brenda. I don't want you to be soaked too." He seemed to understand, as he bounded off toward the house.

Chance was there at the front door when Charlotte arrived.

"It's raining," he said. He was standing there, offering an umbrella. She was coming in rather than going out, but she didn't take the time to make a wisecrack about her brother offering her an umbrella under those circumstances. She couldn't resist a jab about the rain, though.

"Brilliant deduction," she responded. "I did notice that. In fact, I'm dripping all over this nice marble floor."

"It's a precursor for the hurricane. For Charlie," Chance said. "We've been listening to the news. The hurricane is about to hit the coast, and the projections now have it coming right over our heads by Monday night. There apparently is a thunderstorm running just ahead of it and in this direction."

"The curse of Charlotte?" she asked. "I guess you're going to blame this on me."

"Most certainly," Chance asked. "You are carrying two rifles." He said it as if Charlotte didn't know she was.

"I've armed myself from those blaming me for Hurricane Charlie hitting here. I suppose you're going to tell me that it's missing Hilton Head Island altogether."

"By nearly 100 miles," Chance said, a smug tone to his voice.

"Make yourself useful, Chance. Do you think you could get these rifles stashed in the trunk of your car without anyone seeing you do it? I'd like to take them out of the field of play. You can make having that umbrella in your hand meaningful."

"Aye, aye, Captain," he said, with a smile.

"I'm serious, Chance. I think there was just an attempt on Brenda's life, and I think I may know why."

The grin disappeared from her brother's face. "Sure, I'll take care of that."

"I'm going up to our room now," Charlotte said. And then she assured him she and Brenda would be safe when he showed concern about that. "I suggest you find Marilyn and the two of you keep close to your room, though."

As she reached the landing to the second floor, she heard the rustling of material and her eye caught movement behind a column.

"Come on out, Clea," she said. "I don't think we've met yet—at least not since I was in college at Elon with Regina—but it looks like we'll be up here together for a few more days at least."

"Is it true that you are a police woman?" Clea, swirling into view in her dark blue silken robes and red turban, asked in a soft singsong voice.

"I was FBI, but I'm retired," Charlotte said.

"But Regina said you were here to save us."

"Did she now? Do you know where Regina is hiding?"

"There's little mystery there. But I wouldn't be too taken by what Regina says and does. She's not quite right in the head. She never is able to reveal anything directly."

Do tell; it seems to be a family trait, Charlotte thought, but what she said was, "No, I'm not too worried about where Regina is—as long as she stays there. What is it that you think the family needs saving from?"

"As always, the Fowlers need to be saved from themselves," Clea answered enigmatically. "Are you coming to the séance tonight? Tell me that you'll be there."

"Certainly we'll be there, unless there is any other entertainment on for the evening," Charlotte said. She added, "Will you tell me all this evening?"

But Clea had already swirled away, with Charlotte discovering upon looking behind the column that there was a door there to a servants' stairway.

She was to learn that evening that Regina wasn't the only one of the Fowler cousins who couldn't convey information directly.

* * * *

The rain was still just a sprinkle but the wind was noticeably picking up when they all gathered for predinner drinks in the main drawing room. Or, rather, all beyond the ever-absent Regina had gathered but Samantha, who didn't put in an appearance, although they all could clearly see her on the terrace beyond the French doors in the drawing room. Wearing a beige trench coat and carrying a large flashlight, she was looking up at the sky intently, as if waiting for it to fall. She was standing backed by an eerie light coming from somewhere beyond her to the south.

Charlotte found herself standing beside Sydney, with both looking at Samantha through the glass of the patio doors. Brenda, Marilyn, and Chance were over at a bookcase stuffed with knick-knacks, and Marilyn was taking objects off the shelf to admire them. Clea and her husband were standing apart. She was in something of a trance state and swaying slightly. Rupert had his hand on her arm to keep her steady. He had a weary "she does this all the time" expression on his face, and he looked around the room to see who was watching her. Janice and Curtis were picking their way through the residents and guests with trays of stemmed glasses of white and red wine and flutes of something sparkly, which, having tried it, Charlotte decided was several dollars a glass short of real champagne.

Charlotte mentally added "waitress" to Janice's dogsbody jobs around here. She really was a rather mousey-looking young woman, Charlotte thought. Maybe an isolated glorified go-for job like this suited her, although there must be something of interest to her to stick it out here with these three crazy cousins. As Charlotte looked closer at Janice, she thought she noticed something for the first time. She probably was the only one who noticed who didn't already know, she thought. Janice was the sort of woman who didn't get many second looks. Charlotte pushed the observation to the back of her mind—for possible relevance to something later.

While Charlotte's crew chatted away among themselves, and Clea and her husband practiced their regal statue act, Sydney slid in beside Charlotte to talk to her in private. She got in a question, however, before he could voice the one she knew was coming.

"Samantha looks ghastly with that light behind her. Where is it coming from, do you know? It's too cloudy for a sunset, which would come from a different direction anyway."

"Those are the lights from the airstrip," Sydney said. "I told you about it. Samantha insisted we get it put in first—and that it have a first-rate lighting system."

"You anticipate night landings here?"

Sydney shrugged. "It all looks good on paper to prospective investors who are of the class to have their own airplanes. Samantha tests the lights nearly every night. Obsessive woman."

"Yes, she is, isn't she?" Charlotte said. "Rather dangerous too, I think."

That brought Sydney to the topic he was dying to ask about. "Do you really think she's done something with Regina? Have you had any luck in finding her? I certainly haven't."

"No, Sydney, I don't actually think Samantha has done Regina in—although how the two have survived with each other over the years is beyond me. I think the real question is what Regina has done—and is waiting for—to cause herself to disappear. And I wonder what you know about that." She looked expectantly at Sydney, but he didn't satisfy her curiosity.

Showing confusion, whether feigned or genuine—Sydney had always been a consummate actor in such matters, Charlotte thought—he said, "I'm just trying to stay low profile here and get a job done that my wife wants finished. I'm not involved in anything questionable or illegal."

"For the moment?" Charlotte asked. "Laying low? Have you not resolved all of your legal issues with the authorities?"

"Yes, of course I have," Sydney answered.

"Why did you change your name to Fowler? Does that give you a chance to duck under a reputation you'd otherwise have with these investors you are talking about—and, perhaps, keep you out of the gun sights of Gloria's Mafia relatives?"

Sydney blushed and muttered something about all men marrying into the Fowler family being expected to take on the Fowler name. Before he could say anything further, Curtis was standing at the double doors between the drawing room and the main dining room, ringing a bell, and announcing that dinner was served.

At the sound of food being in the offing, Clea came out of her trance. She looked over to Marilyn and, seeing that Charlotte's sister-in-law was holding a small, worn wooden music box, called out, "Isn't that interesting, my dear? Since you have gravitated to that, why don't you put it aside for our séance later this evening? I always use an object like that—something that has caught the attention of someone at the séance—to help me bring up the spirits wanting to cross to us."

"I was just—" Marilyn said, looking like she'd been caught trying to shoplift the box.

"Please, it's how Clea works," Rupert said. "Just put it there, on that table, and I'll see that it gets to the séance. Now, shall we go in? I think senior guests first—Dr. and Dr. Diamond? And then, umm, Ms. Diamond and Ms. Brandon, not being able to help himself from using Brenda's stage name. Umm, OK, together, if you wish, I suppose. Then Clea and me and, last of all . . . whatshisname."

Charlotte didn't need any more than Rupert saying that and the venomous looks he and Sydney exchanged to know how the brother-in-laws felt toward each other.

It was no surprise that Curtis and Janice served the meal, and in formal style. The food was surprisingly good. This was somewhat surprising to Charlotte, who did quite a bit of picking through it, without success, trying to find evidence of the rabbits Rupert had bagged earlier in the day.

Charlotte wondered whether Samantha would eat the food on offer as well and, if so, where. She certainly was making clear how she viewed the presence of guests Regina had invited here for the week. Charlotte had no intention of spending a week here, if she could manage to avoid it. She thought she had a handle on the Elon College issue—and at least an inkling of the drug case issue Evan had asked her to explore. Other mysteries were negligible, she thought. She certainly didn't worry about Regina's absence; she welcomed it.

Clea, with Rupert sitting close to her, clucking, and cutting up her food for her, ate like she was preparing to run a marathon and surprise the world. And, perhaps she *was* preparing herself to surprise the world.

* * * *

The setting came right out of a B movie, and Brenda was smiling from ear to ear. With a storm raging outside and the lights flickering, everyone was ushered into a room in the deep recesses of the building that was decorated to be the epitome of what a Victorian England clairvoyant's parlor would have been like. Sydney had warned Charlotte and her group what they would find.

"Fowler's Folly was a spiritualist colony's retreat for a couple of decades," he said. "Clea held sway as one of their primary clairvoyants, and this was the center of her—and their—world. I'm told that Frederick was better at it but that Clea was the one who used all of the traditional trappings."

Looking around at the walls draped in heavy scarlet velvet; the multicolored carpet on the floor; the honeycombed ceiling in a somber, dark wood; the heavy, circular mahogany table in the center, with eight chairs pulled up to it, and the flickering chandelier hanging low over the center of the table, Charlotte's thoughts went to how the room must be set up for the table to levitate at command and apparitions to appear and then evaporate in a mist of smoke. Naturally, she thought, Clea was seated at the table already, in a half trance.

The seat with all the controls under the table edge, Charlotte mused. And maybe with the help of Rupert.

"Isn't it just too perfect?" Brenda murmured to her as they entered the room. She gave a little shudder of pleasure.

"Exactly," Charlotte muttered back. "Just too, too perfect."

"Go with it, Charlotte," Chance whispered. "It could be fun. And there's nothing else going tonight with this storm. The electricity will have gone out before we could find something in the library we'd want to read. We could learn something."

82

There was that, Charlotte thought. She had theories for most of what she needed to know—and God knew she wanted them to be able to get out of here as soon as possible. Something told her that Clea might be the key to being sure.

"Is this the hurricane already hitting?" Marilyn asked as she belatedly entered the room.

"No," Sydney offered. "This is just the thunderstorm running in front of the hurricane from the east. As we're at the top of the mountains, we get the full effect of it. I certainly hope that Regina—"

"Excuse me, Master Rupert," Curtis said from the doorway. "With the storm tonight and the hurricane coming, I've sent all but the cook, the handyman, and a kitchen maid and an upstairs maid home until after the hurricane has passed. The ones remaining will room in the house. I hope that meets with your approval. I couldn't find Ms. Samantha to consult with her. Janice and I will serve drinks and then withdraw as well, if that suits."

Rupert, who was standing behind Clea's chair and motioning for the others to sit where they wanted, inclined his head in assent.

"Everyone take a drink quickly, please. Clea is ready to begin," he commanded.

Clea certainly looked like she was ready to begin. She was already in a trance, her eyes closed and her head revolving slightly. She was humming from deep in her chest. The table was wide, with a white silken cloth on it that went to the floor—just as Charlotte assumed it would to hide whatever mechanics were in play under the table. Her arms were extended on the top of the table, her hands encircling and lightly touching the small wooden music box Marilyn had been looking at in the drawing room. From somewhere, the source cleverly concealed, as Charlotte knew it would be, a beam of light illuminated the box. Candles also were set on the table, throwing light on the box. Charlotte was glad they were there, as the flickering chandelier didn't promise to last very long. Of course, it was flickering more dramatically than the lights in the rest of the house had been doing as they moved to the séance room, so Charlotte assumed the flickering here was for effect.

Everyone settled, the drinks served, and Curtis and Janice having withdrawn, Rupert sat in the chair to the right of Clea. Clea's humming became more pronounced and there was a hint of eerie music elsewhere in the room as well—the source of which seemed to move from place to place along the walls.

All those gathered joined hands to create an unbroken circle around the table, as if knowing this was expected. There was an empty chair, but all had probably heard enough about the séance style to know that there would be—to show welcome to whatever spirit the clairvoyant conjured up for the session. Such light as there was in the room dimmed even more, although the light on the music box intensified. The box also began to move, as if on its own, and to rise an inch above the table top.

"And we have liftoff," Charlotte murmured in sotto voce under the gasps that Marilyn and Brenda emitted. Brenda's gasp seemed to be edged with amusement, though, and she nudged Charlotte with her shoulder. Charlotte wanted to say that Brenda could nudge her with a shoulder any time she wanted, but Charlotte did want to see how this would play out, so she settled down.

She even suppressed a snort when the table itself rose off the floor about an inch. The hydraulics worked fine with nary a squeak, she thought.

"Please close your eyes tightly and concentrate on welcoming thoughts," Rupert directed.

Umm, OK, maybe, Charlotte thought as she complied.

"Come to us, spirit of the evening," Clea was murmuring in a high-pitched, singsong voice. "The people of Fowler's Retreat are confused and seek enlightenment. This music box has called out to us. What does it have to say to us?"

"I am here." A deeper, gruff, mournful voice. Even Charlotte jerked a bit at this unexpected sound. Coming out of Clea, surely. But nothing like the way Clea would talk. Not the way anyone at the table would talk. Maybe a voice as low as Rupert's. But no sign of accent.

"Who is here? Who is with us?" Clea's query.

"The father of the spawn of the family. One who tried to drown the bad seed but who paid the price for it. Do not ask further."

Charlotte had cracked her eyes. Yep, despite the lighting—obviously on purpose—she saw Rupert's mouth move slightly as the "visitor" spoke.

"Tell us of the danger still with us," Clea pleaded. "Tell us through the story of the music box."

"Two children, the spawn and the companion from the servant's quarters. Sammy and Jay. Playing in the forest behind the replica house. Sammy hiding a music box in the cleft of a tree, sharing the secret only with Jay. Sammy has no friend other than Jay. Certainly not me, knowing now that the incident in the river was no accident, but an attempt to save the world from evil spawn.

"Jay knows what Sammy is and has done and knows why the opium has been hidden in the box and in the tree. The secret cannot be kept. I had taken opium before the shot. The house was searched high and low as the packet was not found with me. Could someone else have take it away? Could it be that I had not done this myself? I screamed the truth, but they could not see me; could not hear me. They found the music box, ravished by its nights in the wood. The spawn drew in breath as they opened it to see what was inside—to find it empty. From the hallway,

Jay's eyes met Sammy's. He had protected Sammy. The opium he sold in—"

A noise, a far off hollow-sounding banging, intervened over the voice of the apparition and the hint of music in the room. It had been there earlier, but Charlotte, and perhaps the rest, had taken it as the banging of a loose shutter on the side of the house in the storm. But the sound of the storm had suddenly stopped. In contrast the hollow sound of the banging had not.

Clea, clearly irritated, changed gears. "Where have you gone? Come back to us."

There only was silence. Those around the table had started to fidget, but Rupert, in his English accent, admonished them to be still—that Clea would have to withdraw from the trance slowly or she would be ill from the effects.

But Clea didn't withdraw from the spell. She whispered. "Who is there? Someone else wanting to speak with us, help us in our need."

"I am here." This time a woman's voice. Not the one Clea was using in her trance, though.

"What do you wish to convey to us?" Spoken by Clea.

"My family. My husband. My daughter. Where have they gone? What are they doing? I fear they may bring harm—that they may be lost in the process."

Charlotte didn't wait any longer. She pulled the hand of Brenda from her right and Chance from her left and joined them, pulling herself out of the circle. Both Brenda and Chance slitted their eyes to see what she was doing, but she placed a finger to her mouth and silently pulled away from the table and glided out of the room. In the foyer she stopped, trying to locate where the dull sound of hammering was coming from.

She mounted the stairs to the landing, moved behind columns, and opened the door to the servants' staircase that Clea had used earlier in the day to accomplish her disappearing act.

The sound was coming from below, echoing up the stairwell shaft—most certainly in a louder tone than whoever was doing the hammering below assumed. Charlotte descended the stairs into the dimly lit basement and felt her way toward the sound, which, when she slid into the room, proved to be the wine cellar.

An empty wine rack had been pulled away from the stone wall, and Curtis was whacking on the stones with a mallet muffled with a cloth. Obviously the sound wasn't as muffled as he thought it was. Janice was standing next to him, holding up a lit lantern to beam light on where he was pounding. He'd already gotten a couple of stones out of the wall. The light of the lantern revealed that there was a space behind the wall.

"Found any treasure?" Charlotte asked, startling them and causing them both to turn horrified faces to Charlotte—faces that showed identical and unusually shaped noses. The two of them had turned just right in close profile to Charlotte earlier in the evening to permit her—highly trained in facial recognition—to figure out that they were father and daughter.

A half hour later, the two had willingly gone to an interior room without windows, where Sydney and Chance were set guarding the only door to the corridor, while Charlotte called the police down in Waynesboro below the western slope of the mountains.

"They're coming right up," she announced to the group, gathered now in the drawing room.

"How did you know?" Marilyn asked.

Charlotte looked over to Clea, who was sitting on a sofa, with Rupert standing behind her, his hands possessively on her shoulders. Clea was giving a Cheshire Cat expression. Charlotte wasn't finished with the game Clea was playing, though, so she just shrugged and said, "I could see that they were father and daughter and I figured that the vandalism going on in the house wasn't random and probably was an inside job. I was just following where my intuition and training led me."

Brenda was about to follow up with another question, when Charlotte's cell phone rang and she answered it. After she rang off, she turned to the group. "So much for the police coming up tonight. They've tried and the road is washed out. The cuts into the embankment to widen the road have given way in a couple of places and mud slides have covered the road. We're stuck up here until Monday at least—no matter whether they get a bulldozer in to clear the roads or can line up a helicopter to fly in."

At that moment, one of the French doors to the terrace flew open, and a soaked and crazed-looking Samantha took two steps into the room.

Charlotte gave her a look of disgust, took Brenda's hand, and said, "Brenda and I are retiring from the night. I suggest you do the same, Marilyn. Go to Chance and tell him they can take the guard off Curtis and Janice. No one's going anywhere tonight. But I suggest we all lock our doors."

Clea looked up and said in a somewhat faraway voice, "Should we continue tomorrow? With the séance?"

Brenda looked at Charlotte with surprise as Charlotte answered, "You bet we should continue with the séance tomorrow. There's nothing that I want more tomorrow than to talk to this apparition of yours again."

"What the hell—?" Samantha started to speak for the first time. But Charlotte cut her off.

"I'll let Clea and Rupert fill you in on whatever version they want to tell you," she said to Samantha. "Be advised that Brenda and I are locking our door tonight—and that we have a highly attentive dog in the room with us. Only one, though, because the other one will be with Marilyn and Chance."

And with that, she latched onto Brenda and left the room.

Chapter Six: Treasure, Quandary, and Danger

The soft knock on the bedroom door early Sunday morning woke Charlotte, who, due to her statuesque frame, typically found it hard to find a comfortable sleeping position and thus was a light sleeper. Brenda was a dead-to-the world sleeper, so the tap on the door had no effect on the slightly musical sound of her deep breathing. Sam, who was stretched out on the end of the bed sat up and pricked his ears, but he didn't growl or bark, so Charlotte knew it was a "friend" doing the knocking.

She sat up on the side of the bed, pulled the sleeping robe around her that had come off in the intimate moments of the previous night, and went to the door.

"I'm taking Rocket for a walk and presume Sam needs one too," Chance whispered when she opened the door to him. He was dressed and Rocket obviously was ready to go. Sam bounded off the bed and joined his canine comrade in the hall, so he obviously was eager to take a stroll outside too.

"I have a better idea," Charlotte answered in a low voice. "If you'll stand guard out here in the hall, I'll get dressed and take the dogs. There's something I want to check. Is it storming outside?" She and Brenda had had the heavy drapes pulled over the window. They quite effectively had blotted out any sound from the outside in the night. That had helped to keep Sam from fidgeting.

"No, it's quite calm—eerily so. The calm between the storms, I think, although I heard on my radio that there's another storm between us and the hurricane that's on the way. The gods obviously aren't pleased we're on vacation. The hurricane is still predicted to go over us later this evening according to the radio, and it's still a big one."

"Where's Marilyn? I don't like the idea of her being alone in your room. There's all sorts of danger lurking about."

"I do get that vibe, yes," Chance said. "Marilyn talked until she dozed off about ghosts stalking the corridors. Wasn't that séance something last night? Were you serious when you said you wanted that crazy lady to do another one?"

"Absolutely, yes. We have to have another séance. Is Marilyn still asleep?"

"Oh, she's up already and down in the kitchen. She thought the cook would need help in feeding this bunch. She says the place makes her feel creepy even during the day and she'd rather have something practical and familiar to do—and someone working beside her."

Charlotte's outing with the dogs took her to check out the airstrip, finding it finished and ready for use. The atmosphere was even more eerie than Chance had described it—deathly silent. Not even the birds were twittering. She realized that meant the birds had probably deserted the mountaintop, a sure sign of the intensity of the hurricane that was approaching. "The hurricane I'm summoning, if you believe family legend," she said to no one in particular. The Fowler family wasn't the only one steeped in family legends, although the Diamond family

91

ones were decidedly tame against what the Fowlers could conjure up.

This led her to thinking of—and reassessing—the youngest of the Fowler cousins, Clea. They were all crazy, including Clea, but each in her own way and each as crazy as a fox.

The airstrip was a grass field, but one that had been carefully graded, hardened, and kept close cropped and with a landing surface long enough to take a corporate prop plane. Probably not long enough for any size jet, though. This surprised Charlotte, as the investors Sydney talked about trying to interest would be more likely to fly jets than prop planes. The field did, indeed, have a set of landing lights. She didn't go all the way to the landing strip, though, but stayed in the protection of a line of trees, because she could see Samantha out on the strip picking up small branches and other debris from the previous night's storm.

"So, what is she expecting?" Charlotte asked the dogs. Some prospective investors already? Is that why she was being so rude about having Charlotte and her crew here? But the dogs, as eager as they were to talk to Charlotte, didn't seem to know the answer to the questions she was asking. At least they didn't make an attempt to answer her in English. "And why did the landing strip have to be finished and ready for use before the house itself was in the condition to be shown to prospective investors? Hmmm—not to mention why was Samantha picking up degree now, when there's another thunderstorm coming, with a hurricane right behind it?"

She kept an eye on the ruins of the replica house as she returned to the main house, but she discerned nothing out of the ordinary in that direction. Still, she stopped while they were in the center of the meadow triangulated by the main house, the replica house ruins, and the line of trees into the forest where Brenda had nearly been shot the day before and placed a cell phone call. Professor Chafin, down in Elon, confirmed the suspicion Charlotte had phoned her about the previous day. "What should we do from here?" Chafin asked.

"No one up here is going anywhere until somebody comes for us," Charlotte told the interim college president. "You should have enough for an arrest warrant. Have whoever you're working with transfer that over to the Waynesboro police and they can serve it when they get up here—which I hope will be tomorrow morning."

Back at the house, rather than going to the main dining room, where the others would be gathering for breakfast, Charlotte went up to the third floor of the east wing that obviously had been a servants' area and, equally obviously, hadn't enjoyed the effects of the renovations yet. A service flat here, with two small bedrooms and a bath off a central sitting room was where Curtis and Janice had been locked in the previous night after the storm had gone through.

She took the key off a table a distance down the corridor from the door to the sitting room and knocked lightly on the door before unlocking it and entering. She had Sam and Rocket with her and so felt protected enough. Besides, she didn't read the two thieves as being physical threats.

They were sitting on chairs opposite from each other and apparently had both just been staring into space. They turned listless gazes on her when she entered. She walked over and placed the room key on top of a bureau before coming back to face them.

"I know you are aware that another storm and a hurricane are coming and the authorities won't be up here until they are past us. You also know that the road down the mountain is blocked by landslides in several places. I see no need to keep you locked up, and you're free to come down to take your breakfast in the kitchen. I'm sure you both know this house better than anyone else and could escape it if you wanted to—if you want to risk trying to work your way down the mountain on foot—we've been to your rooms and confiscated all of your shoes—in a hurricane. You'd then only have a short time of freedom before the police picked you up anyway."

"We have no intention of trying to escape," Curtis said in a weary voice.

"I thought both of you looked smarter than to be blindly poking around the house looking for gold based on some crazy legend," Charlotte said.

"We weren't just poking blindly around the house," Janice answered with spirit, "and the legend isn't crazy."

"Janice," Curtis said, reaching over and touching her arm to restrain her. But then he sat back in his chair and sighed. "What's the use. Janice is right. The search wasn't haphazard. We had maps of built-in hiding places."

"Maps from where?" Charlotte asked.

"My grandfather was the last in a succession of architects of this house," Curtis answered. "He built in hiding places to Franklin Fowler's specifications. And he kept a copy of the map for himself. And it's a good thing he did. We were just seeing that he got justice—that our family got what the Fowlers owed us."

"Justice?" Charlotte asked.

"He never got paid for the work he did for the Fowlers," Janice said, her voice vehement. "Franklin Fowler and his wife got killed out West in a train wreck. Nothing in writing on a contract with my father was left behind. So, he didn't get paid for putting the finishing touches on the house. We were just taking back what was due him."

"But if the legend of the treasure is just that . . . you've obviously been poking here and there and come up empty handed."

"What makes you think we've come up empty handed?" Curtis said in a tone of defiance and smiling for the first time that morning. "There was something tucked away in every place we looked. We haven't come away empty handed. You stopped me when I'd just gotten the crevice in the wine cellar open last night. Go check for yourself. I bet you'll find something there. Not a huge treasure in itself, but a piece of one."

And indeed, when she looked, Charlotte did find something in the crevice of the wine cellar wall—a small gold bar, with the initials FF on it. Just the one bar, but undoubtedly valuable if it was the pure gold it looked like it was.

When she came up the stairs and decided to check in on the activity in the dining room, she was surprised and shocked to see Chance there—but not Brenda.

"Chance! I thought you were on guard duty in the bedroom wing hallway. Is Brenda down here with you?"

"She popped out of the room and told me to go ahead to the dining room. She's not down yet."

"Shit," Charlotte said, as she did an about face and headed for the staircase in the foyer. She realized she hadn't told Brenda or Chance of her deep suspicion that Brenda was in danger. She hadn't wanted to alarm them, but better that she had. It was her fault.

As she moved quickly up the stairs, she used all of her powers of observation. And it was a good thing she did, because the strong cord that had been stretched across the top step of the lower staircase blended in almost perfectly with the veined Carrara marble of the steps and banister. She found how it was attached and got it pulled away just as Brenda, smiling and cheery, reached the landing below the stained glass portrait of the unfortunate Claudia Fowler and turned to face Charlotte, who had just raised to a standing position.

The "dear, dear, Charlotte" greeting and the embrace and sweet kiss told Charlotte this wasn't the moment to tell Brenda of the danger she surely was in, but it was appropriate for Charlotte to tell her, "Stay close to me while we're here. I don't want you out of my sight again."

"How sweet . . . and romantic," Brenda said, flashing one of her signature melting smiles.

"Something like that," Charlotte muttered. "Shall we go to breakfast? I want Clea to give us another séance performance before the next storm hits."

Marilyn, the cook, and the kitchen maid had laid out a breakfast spread fit for royalty on the buffet table in the dining room for everyone to help themselves to. And everyone was there now that Charlotte and Brenda had entered the room—including Samantha, who had prepared a plate and was sitting at the dining room table as normally as you please, giving no excuse or acknowledgement that she had been avoiding everyone for over a day.

Charlotte scanned those at the table from the Fowler household—Samantha, Clea, Rupert, and Sydney—for any sign of disappointment that Brenda had made it to the dining room. But no one was looking guilty. She went to the door into the kitchen. Curtis, Janice, the upstairs maid—and now the cook and kitchen maid as well—were all seated at the large kitchen table, tucking into their own meals.

Charlotte waved Brenda to a seat between Chance and Marilyn and she, herself sat down directly across from Samantha. "I'm sure you've heard that we're trapped up here until they can get the road open or a helicopter in here, Samantha," she said. "But I'm sure you'll be relieved that the Diamonds, Brenda, and I will move on as soon as we can."

"Oh, there's no hurry. Stay as long as you like. I thought Regina said you'd be here for a week."

Well, now, that's quite a reversal of attitude, Charlotte thought, but it isn't what she said. What she said was, "Speaking of Regina, I haven't seen her since we got up here. Do you have any idea where she is?"

"Regina's just being Regina," Samantha answered in a breezy tone. "She's around here somewhere. I'm sure she has her reasons for being reclusive, not that I care much what they are. I, for one, am enjoying her absence."

At least you know Regina really well, Charlotte thought, as she tucked into her breakfast, working her mind to decide just which of the delicacies she could risk Brenda's frown to restock her plate with.

Chapter Seven: Clea's Continued Explosive Trances

The same set of attendees as the night before gratefully fled to the insulated cocoon of the séance parlor an hour after lunch to escape watching the inevitability of the arrival of another thunderstorm followed by Hurricane Charlie, the coming of which was announced by the whistling of the wind and the descending of darkness. As Clea was maneuvering Marilyn into choosing from a cigarette table in the drawing room a wafer-thin, embossed miniature pill box in the shape of a pumpkin for a séance catalyst, all of their heads popped up at the flash of light beyond the French doors onto the terrace to the west. The storm was coming in from the southeast, so they knew that it looked even more ominous from the other side of the house. The wind hadn't brought in thunder and lightning yet, and it wasn't doing so now. The lights to the landing strip had turned on. Samantha, swathed in a slick mackintosh, the mere trench coat of the previous day not having given her sufficient protection, was seen powering herself against the wind across the terrace, presumably headed toward the lights.

Before anyone could question out loud what she was doing or suggest that someone go after her, Rupert was at the door to the foyer announcing that the séance was about to begin and that they all were to follow him. Clea had already slipped out of the drawing room and was in place when they all arrived in the velvet-draped inner room. They probably would have searched out a room like this in which to ride out the storm even if the séance hadn't been planned.

The beaten-silver pill box was already in place, in front of where Clea, eyes slitted almost closed, swaying a bit in her chair, and humming to herself, was sitting. As with the music box the evening before, a beam of light picked the pill box out. Charlotte pointedly was the last to sit, and, as she did so, she took the gold bar she'd found in the wine cellar out of a pocket and slammed it sharply on the table in front of her.

Everyone around the table looked at the bar with surprise. Clea's eyes opened to take it in as well, but she didn't seem as surprised as the rest. Inclining her head and giving Charlotte a slight smile, she gave a terse nod, thus confirming to Charlotte that Clea had already been wise to the father/daughter thief act and that her last "in touch" with the spirits last evening had been to clue Charlotte in to that. Charlotte had decided to watch what Clea was up to and signaling very closely.

Touching the pill box, Clea slid it gently out of the spotlight as Charlotte pushed the gold bar to the middle of the table. Clea looked over at Rupert and nodded, and he leaned across the table and moved the gold bar into the lit circle the pill box had vacated.

As the night before, all joined hands and were asked to close their eyes, and concentrate on clearing the atmosphere for the smooth passage of a spirit into the room.

"I must speak," a muffled, deep-timbre voice was heard to say. It was the same male voice of the first trance on the previous evening.

"We have cleared a passage for you. Speak to us. Tell us of the gold." Clea's clairvoyant role singsong voice.

"It is mine. The gold is mine. I placed it. I will have it for eternity."

"But we have stopped the thieves who were stealing it from you," Clea answered. "We thought you would be content now."

"I'll not be content until treacherous flesh of my flesh is stopped," the gruff voice angrily growled. "Mere misguided fools don't worry me. Maps can deceive. Crumbs can be planted to hide cake. Fools miss large by being blinded by small and think large when they should think small. It's the greed of my own cake-obsessed flesh, which must be stopped. I want—"

The whole house was jolted by a lightning strike on the roof and the opening of the skies in a deluge, the sound of which drowned out the background music in the room. The chandelier flickered and died. Everyone in the room counted in their mind the seconds before they'd been told to trust that a generator would come on. And then it did. The next storm had arrived in full force.

And when it did, it revealed Clea standing at the table, arms raised. "I cannot work like this," she screamed. "This séance is suspended. Be gone from my presence, all of you."

Chairs shuffled and attendees rose and moved out of the room, seeking a position that would combine safety with an opportunity to observe the fury of the thunderstorm preceding Hurricane Charlie that was descending on them. Only Clea, Rupert, and Charlotte remained standing at their positions at the table for several more seconds. Clea nodded to Charlotte and Charlotte nodded back, turned, and crossed the foyer into the drawing room, where most of the rest were gathering just a few steps back from the French doors out onto the western terrace, standing far enough inside the doors not to be hit by broken glass if the wind caved the doors in, but close enough to observe the unleashing fury of the storm. Sam and Rocket were not so afraid; they were sitting on their haunches, their bodies trembling with excitement, and their noses plastered to the glass of the French doors.

As Charlotte arrived, all jerked at the flash of lightning in the meadow beyond and the toppling of a huge, old oak tree at the other side of the clearing as it was struck by the lightning bolt. Miraculously, beyond that, the lights on the landing strip still blazed. The dogs yelped, and, reaching, for their collars, Charlotte pulled Sam and Rocket back from the glass.

Brenda turned to Charlotte and said, "Did you see what the lightning did to that tree?" But when she did so, she found Charlotte muttering to herself in contemplation. What she was murmuring was, "Fools miss large by being blinded by small and think large when they should think small."

"Everyone back to the séance room," Rupert appeared at the door from the foyer and commanded. "The full force of the hurricane can't be far behind."

* * * *

The weary residents and guests who had left the séance table at the thunderous sailing over the mountaintop of the lightning storm and the full-force roar of the arriving hurricane returned to their places.

As Rupert ushered them all back to the séance room, Brenda whispered to Charlotte, "I can't understand why you're egging this on. It's obviously all fake. It was fun for a while, but it isn't my idea of a great way to ride out a hurricane."

"But it's very informative if you read between the groans and sighs," Charlotte said. "It still has mysteries to unlock, I think."

As Marilyn passed them in the foyer, she whispered, "Isn't this delicious fun?"

Brenda answered with a, "And very naughty of a minister, I must say."

"I'm on vacation," Marilyn answered back, with a grin. "The dead are big business in my line of work."

Coming up behind them, Sydney wondered out loud how long it would be before they were going through the eye of the hurricane—whether when it was passing directly overhead they should check on Samantha and maybe there would be hope of finding Regina. Chance shrugged. Rupert spoke up. "We will know if there's a lull. The room isn't that insulated. But for now we have unfinished business with the spirits."

"Are you sure?" Chance asked. "Do we really want to continue with this?" He had addressed the question to Charlotte, because Clea, with Rupert standing solicitously behind her chair, had sat down in a drawing room chair, eyes closed, swaying, and in a half trance.

But it was Clea who answered. "Unfinished business. We must bring out the troubled spirit one more time."

Chance looked to Charlotte again, who shrugged and said, "Yes, I think we must." That seemed to take care of the question, and the group started shuffling into the séance room and taking their places.

This time, the gold bar had disappeared—with Charlotte making a note to check with both Rupert and Sydney about that later. She had been so intent on watching Clea earlier when the group broke up at the dramatic departure of the thunderstorm and ominous arrival of the hurricane that she hadn't noticed who had taken the gold bar. It belonged to the family, not any single part of it, although Charlotte was getting the sense of the family being whittled down and moving to separate battle stations.

Now the pumpkin-shaped silver pill box was back in the beam of light, a beam that pulsed with the sound of the generator at the side of the house that was giving it life.

Rupert gave his usual instructions to those sitting around the table, and Clea went into her customary descent into the world of the dead, struggling theatrically to conjure up whatever spirit could be drawn out by the silver pill box.

The spirit that faded in with an "I am here," spoke in a refined male voice, a smooth baritone.

At Charlotte's side, Brenda gave a little lurch, her hand trembling in Charlotte's grip, and gasped an involuntary, "Frederick."

"Yes, my love," the spirit answered even though Brenda's utterance could hardly have reached across the table.

Bastard, Charlotte thought, but she also had to admire Rupert. Perhaps he should be thinking of a higher calling—Hollywood rather than parlor tricks—maybe voiceovers for animated movies. He and Clea must have prepared hard for this opportunity. Apparently recordings of Frederick Fowler's voice existed. Of course, his movies probably could be found on late night TV, thanks to Brenda having appeared in them as well.

"What does this object tell us?" Clea begged of the spirit.

"A tale of treachery lodged in generosity."

"What is it you see? Describe to us the scene."

"The study. Father's desk." The voice sounded sad, almost mournful. Charlotte could feel Brenda trembling through the hands they were holding. Do *not* feel guilt over that man's death, Brenda, Charlotte screamed in her mind. If she didn't want to know where Clea and Rupert were going with this—didn't need to know—she would have taken Brenda away from here and done everything she could to soothe her spouse's undeserved sense of guilt. Still, at the first mention of unrequited love, she and Brenda would be out of the room regardless of what Charlotte would miss Clea revealing.

"Concentrate," Clea broke in. "The silver pill box. The scene of the silver pill box."

A long sign from the spirit. "Will no one listen to—?"

"First the pill box. Treachery lodged in generosity," Clea insisted. "We must know. We must know the current danger first. The past deception, treachery, and tragedy must wait to safer times. The storm is upon us."

Another deep sigh and that a "Very well. We are in Bangkok, a news room. Sammy is speaking with a woman, a Cambodian. The woman is crying."

"I must resign and take the severance pay." A female's voice, heavily accented. Clea, Charlotte was sure.

"But why? You are one of our most valued reporters." Strangely enough, still a woman's voice. But a different timbre. An American accent. A slightly southern American accent.

Another slight gasp from Brenda. "Regina? Samantha?" she uttered. "Which one?"

"Shush," Charlotte responded. She wanted Brenda innocent to this as long as possible.

"My brother. They will kill him unless I pay off his drug debt. I don't have the funds. I must resign and take the severance pay." The voice of the Cambodian woman.

"Let me think. I believe I know. You may resign and take severance and I will rehire you on contract. But one thing. I will deliver the money myself." The strangely female voice of Sammy. Was Rupert's accent off for once? Was he losing track of who supposedly was talking?

Now the male voice picked up the narrative. "Sammy knows where to go. In the deepest, most vile confines of the Klong Toey Chaophya riverfront, Sammy enters a dark warehouse and is taken to the childhood friend, Jay, moneylender and drug dealer—closest friend before, now, and forever. The ransom paid, Sammy returns to the news bureau, glowing with the treachery couched in generosity that has been bestowed on the Cambodian employee. In gratitude the Cambodian employee opens her hand to reveal the appreciation gift of an exquisitely tooled silver pill box. Ever after . . . but no," the voice now ugly, indignant, "I cannot wait for justice forever. The master's study. The father's desk. The drug provided by the forever friend. The same pistol. Father and son. I cannot—"

The voice of the spirit cut off by the sound of the hurricane blowing in full fury a cacophony of *Sturm und Drang*. And over the sound of the replenished storm, another sound. The sound of a thrumming, sputtering airplane engine. Just overhead. Surely skimming just over the roof of Fowler's Folly. And then, total darkness, as the generator died . . . followed by the noise of a huge explosion to the west and near the house.

"Death from the sky. A lingering, sucking death!" the voice of Frederick Fowler cried out, and then total silence within other than the clutching breathing of those in the room. No Clea humming. No subtle background music. No pulsing of a generator. Just the sound of the fury of the hurricane outside the suffocating walls of Fowler's Folly.

Guests and residents clambered over each other to depart the pitch-dark room, seeking the dim light of the foyer and then the drawing room. All were drawn to the French doors in the drawing room, where Sam and Rocket stood on their hind legs against the glass of the doors, scrabbling to get out. Here, after Charlotte and Brenda had drawn the dogs back, all took in the spectacle of a towering blaze beyond the still-smoldering felled oak tree. The blaze made all the more terrifying by the darkness over the landing strip, the lights of the field having gone out at the same time the generator died and the house went dark.

Chapter Eight: Tying of the Threads

"It's a particularly convoluted case of unbridled greed—on all parts—overriding a willingness to share in a good thing. After decades of being barely able to keep the house from falling down around their ears, when the cousins faced the opportunity for all to prosper, they each wanted it all. Of course, there are large helpings of embezzlement and noxious crime on the side."

Charlotte, Brenda, Marilyn, and Sydney were standing in the meadow between the house and the landing strip, where a large helicopter had landed. They were watching as firemen with chainsaws worked to move branches of the downed oak tree off the body of Samantha Fowler. Others were at the northern end of the strip, still dousing the licks of flames around the small one-engine plane that had slightly overshot the landing strip when the lights went out the previous night and had slammed into the edge of the dense forest, plowing to within a few yards of the Fowler family cemetery.

It had been near dawn before anyone from the house could venture outside in the wake of Hurricane Charlie. Very little damage had been sustained to the house itself, but branches and loose leaves were strewn all over the surrounding grounds. Sam and Rocket, pulling Charlotte along, had been the ones to find Samantha's body, crumpled, soaked, and lifeless, under the oak tree that all had seen go up in flames and topple from the drawing room French doors in the last salvo of thunderstorm before the hurricane set in.

Seeing that she could do nothing to change or help anything, and turning Brenda and Marilyn away from the sight, Charlotte had told Sydney to stay with the body, which was hopelessly pinned under heavy branches, and sent Chance back to the house for blankets to cover the body until the authorities managed to show up. Curtis and Janice were also out, helping to assess the damage and picking up tree limbs and clumps of leaves, but Clea and Rupert had remained in the house.

Clea and Rupert's roles in the drama were over. They had very reason to be pleased with the work they had accomplished.

Charlotte had gone on to the plane crash site, she and the dogs gingerly picking their way through the small patches of fire, fed by the ruptured gas tank of the single-engine, Cessna 152. She'd already figured out—with the help of Regina's original plea for help and Clea's and Rupert's pointed discussions with and for the spirits—that she'd probably find that the plane was delivering illegal drugs, with Samantha Fowler's complicity. And she already was in tune with Evan Worthington's suggestion that the drugs were connected with the palm tree logo operation they had hoped had been shut down south of Charleston and then had doubted. So, she was only mildly surprised— and satisfied—to see packets containing white powder and bearing the logo of the green palm tree strewn around the crash site.

She wasn't at all expecting, though, to find what she did inside the plane. The body of the pilot, killed by the contact with the trees, was still hunched over in the pilot's seat, held up by his seat harness. In shock, Charlotte recognized him instantly, but she searched for identification. That confirmed what she already knew, even though it was entirely unexpected even if it fit in with the circumstances. The dead pilot was Jason Gordon—the palm tree case float plane pilot who had been arrested in Charleston and later escaped from prison. And, as Charlotte now knew, the "Jay" of the stories that Clea spun in the séances just as Samantha was the "Sam" of those stories.

Clea and Rupert clearly had been handholding Charlotte toward the knowledge of what Samantha and her long-time boyfriend, Jason Gordon, were up to on top of this mountain.

Charlotte had been getting there on her own, but the knowledge that what had been going on here was even more convoluted than she had reasoned caused Charlotte to pull away from the crash and work hard to bring her breathing back to normal. Sensing her tension, both Sam and Rocket had come in close to her and rubbed their bodies against her legs in concern. When she gained her composure—thanks largely to the support of her "boys," Charlotte pulled her cell phone out of a pocket and called, first, the Waynesboro police, to let them know they had more of a job up here than just the arrest of a couple of vandals, and then Evan Worthington to report on what she now hoped truly was the end of the palm tree logo drug case.

"So, Samantha was part of a drug distribution network and her interest in this resort deal was just to have a private landing strip up here to receive the drug shipments?" Benda asked. "Why did she allow us to be up here then, when she was expecting a flight? And why did she change her mind on us being up here? At first she was rude and obviously didn't want us here, but yesterday, at breakfast, she said she wanted us to stay the week."

"Regina didn't really give Samantha an opportunity to disagree with having us up here, and Sydney told me the two fought tooth and nail about that before we appeared. As far as changing her mind. I didn't want to tell you, but, at some point, she wanted more time and better opportunity to kill you."

"Kill me? Excuse me?" Brenda gave Charlotte a startled look, staggered a bit, and had to be caught by Marilyn and Sydney, who both were looking equally startled.

"She ultimately wanted to kill everyone in her way to cashing in on this property," Charlotte answered. "Clea's spirits told us she wasn't beyond resorting to murder, and I know Jason Gordon, who apparently has been Samantha's sidekick since childhood, wasn't above it either. Clea and Rupert's little act was claiming Samantha killed both her father and brother and made it look like the Fowler men were prone to suicide. It was all to clear the path for her to wind up with everything. Clea and Rupert obviously were motivated by self-preservation in their efforts to show me what Samantha was doing. And," Charlotte added, a slight smile on her face, "Clean and Rupert want to wind up with everything too."

"But me? Why me?"

"You said she didn't seem to believe that Tony wasn't Frederick's son—or even that you'd actually gotten a divorce from Frederick. She saw you and Tony as a threat to her inheritance here, I believe. The fact that she tried to shoot you at the family cemetery bears that out."

"Tried to shoot me?" Brenda asked, still bewildered.

"Yes. It wasn't Rupert's wayward shooting that almost got you when you were in the cemetery. I went back and found another rifle discarded by the path. I should have wondered why Samantha was wearing gloves when she took you there. She didn't want to leave fingerprints. There have been other swipes at you—ones I didn't tell you about. One I didn't know fit until the rest of the pattern was established. The other night in Elon, after the dinner, when I took the boys for a walk on the road, I almost was run over by a big black sedan, just like the Bentleys over there. I thought it was a careless driver. Later, after you were almost shot, I decided that it was Samantha thinking it was you walking the dogs. Then yesterday morning you were set up for a fall down the stairs coming to breakfast, but I got there and prevented it just before you showed up. What I can't figure out, though, is why she messed with the hoses in Chance's Avalon. If she wanted you where she could get at you, why would she try to make us decide not to come up here?"

Sydney cleared his throat. "Umm, sorry, that was me. But just because I didn't want you getting mixed up in what was going on up here. Regina told me she thought Samantha was doing something with a drug cartel, and I knew if you came up here, Charlotte, you'd get that sorted out. But that almost certainly would have queered the resort deal I was trying to put together. Regina wanted to get rid of Samantha—you're right about all the cousins being at each other's throats over the profits from this deal. And Regina wanted the deal done now. Samantha obviously had more drug business to do and didn't want the place sold until the end of the year. I just wanted this resort deal to go through."

Charlotte glared at her former husband, but before she could say anything, he switched the subject. "You said Samantha would try to kill her cousins. Does that mean she's killed Regina? You haven't really been very helpful on that, Charlotte. I knew you disliked Regina, but—"

"Perhaps the policeman walking up to us will help clear that up," Charlotte said. She turned to two uniformed policeman who had broken away from the two groups by the landing strip—one near the tree being cut away to free Samantha's body and the other over by the crashed plane.

"Hello officers," she said and then identified herself both as a former FBI agent and the one who was in contact with the Waynesboro police and with the acting president of Elon College, who Charlotte had referred to the Waynesboro police.

"A big honcho with the FBI, up in Annapolis, Worthington by name, has been all over us about cooperating with you too," the policeman said, no sign of resentment in his voice or face. "He says it's all connected with an international drug case you were consulting on. So, shoot. What can we do for you?"

"I presume you have the arrest warrant the authorities in Elon were sending to you."

"Yes, ma'am. Do you have any idea where she is?"

"Yes, over in the ruins of that smaller house over there," Charlotte said, gesturing toward the replica of the larger house. "I think I've seen her peeking out from time to time to see what we're up to. While you're in there, you might look around to see if you can find a large amount of gold bullion. If so, it belongs to the wider Fowler family, not just to Regina Fowler. The legendary hidden family fortune. Some of it's going to have to go to Elon College, though."

"I don't understand," Sydney said, baffled, as the policemen strode off toward the replica house. "You've known Regina was in there all along?"

"Yep, I saw her when Samantha shot at Charlotte. She came out of the house enough at the sound of the shooting for me to see her. I figured she'd hold tight there, especially since the road down the mountain is washed out—and that that was the best place for all of us for her to be. I think she's the greediest of the lot. The natural one for you to have latched onto, Sydney. She wanted me up here to bring Samantha and her drug operation down but not to look into what she herself was doing. So, she wanted to keep out of the picture."

"The greediest?" Marilyn asked. Brenda was still looking dazed from the revelation that Samantha had been trying to do her in—and the thought that perhaps Samantha would have tried to get at Tony too and he'd have no idea she was coming at him.

"She had a lot of ill-gotten money at her disposal, although I don't know how much of it she's invested in getting this place fixed up to attract investors. She's walked off with millions from the Elon College endowment fund from when she was on the college's board and had a hand in the school's finances. And, if Clea is to believed, and I think it likely, she has her hands on the famous hidden Fowler treasure trove too. But she's so greedy she didn't just abscond with it; she was staying around here to get her hands on the investors' money as well."

"What do you mean the family treasure trove?" Sydney asked.

"Did you not hear the riddle Clea's spirit gave last evening?" Charlotte said. "'Fools miss large by being blinded by small and think large when they should think small'—everyone, including Curtis and his daughter, Janice, thought the treasure was in the big house, when Franklin cleverly salted just enough there to be found and assumed to be it. In fact, he'd hidden the bulk of it in the replica house where they actually lived while the big house was being built. Regina found it there. And, even with what she had from that, Regina was sticking around for her share of the resort deal. Her greediness did her in. She wanted me up here to get Samantha caught and removed from the equation, but she didn't want me looking into what she was up to—so she removed herself from the house."

"So, Curtis and Janice only found a small part of the treasure," Marilyn said.

"I feel rather sorry for them," Brenda said, "after you told us that Curtis' grandfather had not been paid for his work on the house. What will happen to them, Charlotte?"

"A bit of vandalism, if none of us make a big deal over it," Charlotte answered. She'd already decided not to mention that they'd already found and removed some of the gold bars. She too reasoned that the Fowlers owed them something.

"What about Elon College?" Marilyn asked. "Is it going to close—and now with the embezzlement hanging over its head?"

"This is Virginia," Charlotte answered. "And institutions like Elon College are sacred here. I imagine if Regina cooperates and makes good on what she embezzled—and maybe with interest, which she can do if she's found the Fowler family treasure in the replica house—the problem with the endowment fund will blow over. Those originally pushing for it must have lost a good bit of interest when they found anything left over after expenses went back to the founder's heirs rather than, somehow, into their own pockets. I had Professor Chafin put the auditors on her trail and I hear they have her dead to rights. And the alumnae are coming through with support for keeping the school open, Chafin tells me. The college will probably have to suspend for this coming semester, but then it will be back. We'll still have an alma mater to visit, Marilyn. Regina, I'm sorry to say, will probably also figure out a way to be free and parading as spring queen at the alumnae dinners."

"I didn't know anything about what Regina was up to regarding the college," Sydney said. "I knew nothing except for the part of uncovering Samantha's drug activities, and I thought Samantha deserved getting caught for that. You have to believe me, Charlotte. I really did just want to get this resort deal put through. I'm not involved in any of this other stuff going on up here. Regina didn't even

113

hint to me that she'd embezzled from the college or that she'd found the family's treasure."

"Knowing Regina as I do, I'm inclined to believe you, Sydney," Charlotte answered. "Of course I'd believe you better if you gave back that gold bar you swiped off the séance table last night."

It had only been a hunch, but it shot home. With a muted "Sorry," Sydney took the gold bar out of his pocket and extended it in his hand toward Charlotte.

"No, I suggest you give that to Clea," Charlotte said. "As a good-will offering, in hopes that she keeps you on and lets you benefit from the resort deal. Clea's the surviving cousin in all this—the cousin who won. She gets it all, unless Regina can wriggle herself out of trouble. Clea is the cousin who was considered mousey and with her head in the spirit world. She and Rupert combined to bring the other two down, indirectly, the two of them speaking through the spirits they conjured up for us in the séances. Yes, Sydney, Clea is obviously the smart cookie of the family. I'd suck up to her quickly and well, if I were you."

The six of them—four humans and two happily panting dogs—stood there in contemplation of what Clea, in her manipulation, had accomplished for herself. When they heard approaching footsteps from the direction of the big house, though, they turned to see Chance approaching them.

"I just called down to the rental office in Hilton Head Island," he said when he reached them. "The island was untouched by the hurricane and we still have five days on our house reservation there. If we could just get off this mountain . . ."

"I'm sure they'd helicopter us down to Waynesboro, Charlottesville, or Lynchburg and we could rent a car down there. Rupert could drive the Avalon—oh, I'll have to remember to get the rifles out of the trunk and return Rupert's to him and give the other to the police—down to

Waynesboro and leave it at the garage where his Land Rover is being serviced and drive back up in his car. We can swing by Waynesboro and exchange cars on our way home from Hilton Head. But there's another glitch I see."

"We can take Sam and Rocket, Charlotte," Chance said, immediately understanding what Charlotte was getting at. "There is a pet fee, I discovered, and we'll have to pay for any damage—which these two gentleman won't do any of, I know," he said, bending down and patting each appreciative pouch on the head, "but they can go."

"Thanks, Chance," Charlotte said. "That will make for a perfect vacation, then. That and the good feeling I have that we've finally got this particular drug distribution operation wrapped up. I feel freer than I have for months."

"What will make for a perfect vacation," Chance said, with a laugh, "is that I also checked the weather and there isn't another hurricane forming off the Atlantic coast. If there was, the curse of Charlotte would set in and that's the hurricane that would sweep over Hilton Head Island."

"You're not going to let loose of that family tradition, are you?" Charlotte asked as the others laughed at Chance's joke.

"Did we go to the mountains to avoid a hurricane hitting the coast and get a direct hit by Hurricane Charlie, or didn't we?"

"Touché, Chance, touché. But there's a new family tradition forming. Brenda and I never go on a vacation with you and Marilyn that we don't get embroiled in a complicated mystery."

"Touché to that, little sister, in turn," Chance conceded. "And here's to yet more intriguing combined family vacations."

"Who knows what awaits us at Hilton Head Island," Marilyn chimed in, with Brenda's lilting laugh floating over them in the background.

Who, indeed? What, indeed?

~

Bonus Short Story

Blessedly Cursed Christmas

If how well—or, rather, not well—the Thanksgiving celebration had gone over at the Curtain Call movie colony retirement home was any indication, all of the elaborate preparations and expense going into the Christmas festivities there would go for naught. Not that the retirement community the senior box office leading lady, Brenda Brandon, and her now-spouse, retired FBI agent, Charlotte Diamond, were establishing on the banks of Maryland's Choptank River was anywhere close to a doom-and-gloom nursing home. It was more of a nominal-cost resort, and that had been what Brenda had determined it would be (*Curtain Call*).

When Brenda, known in her childhood home town of Hopewell on the Choptank by her family surname, Boynton, had grown tired of and frustrated by her long, smash-hit run in Hollywood movies and had fled home to Hopewell to virtually hide from the possibility of a murder charge (*Coast to Coast*), she'd had no idea what else in life she wanted to do (*By the Howling*). She was still a beautiful, vibrant woman just past her mid fifties. She certainly didn't know she would meet and fall in love with Charlotte, who had also escaped into early retirement to Hopewell from a highly successful career at the FBI and a failed marriage, had rescued Brenda from the suspicion of murder, and had married her as soon as Maryland opened up to same-sex marriages (*Horrible Honeymoon*).

Brenda had always had in the back of her mind, though, the desire to help and support other actors and production workers in the movie industry, who she considered were the true reason for her own success into a comfortable retirement. So many of them didn't manage to save enough to support themselves when they left the film industry.

She was wealthy in her own right—not just because she had prudently saved while scoring big at the box office but also because she descended from the family that had been the big landowners in the Hopewell area back to before the American Revolution. The magnificent brick Federal-style house she and Charlotte lived in on the banks of the Choptank in Hopewell was the original family plantation house. But her dream of giving back to the workers in the movie world became possible when she won big in the Maryland lottery and a large tract of land became available at the river end of the street she lived on (*What's the Point?*). Charlotte, although far less wealthy, had thrown her lot in with Brenda to develop Curtain Call.

The planned first-phase campus of the community was complete, with only the visitor's guest house to be finished of the second phase. The workers were rushing to complete that before Christmas, although the weather had not been their ally in the effort. And the residents had nearly reached the thirty-resident capacity of the current facility in units that were luxurious suites, not just "rooms." As an added feature, nearly all of the suites boasted a view of the water, which surrounded the peninsula compound on three sides—the Choptank on two sides and a tree-lined marshland and stream running into the Choptank on the third.

This was the second time the community had nearly reached capacity, and it would be the second Christmas since the first residents had arrived. And therein lay the rub of why the Thanksgiving celebration was such a disappointment. The community had been alarmingly depleted the previous Christmas, and this was when the newly minted retirement community administrators had learned a hard lesson of life.

Christmas was some sort of watershed, or goal, for those at the end of their life. For various reasons, in part because winter was a time of vulnerability to colds, flu, and pneumonia, but mostly because the terminally ill tend to hang on to "see another Christmas," an inordinate number of the elderly succumbed in the weeks just following Christmas. Also, unfortunately, although it was a time of joy and hope for many, it was a time of sadness, loneliness, and painful remembrance for others.

After their experience of losing six residents to the ever after during the previous Christmas season, Brenda was determined not to have the same happen this holiday season. She had racked her brain, though, over what she could do. Charlotte had come up with the idea that they had been working on since returning from their late summer vacation at Hilton Head Island (*Fowler's Folly*).

One of the residents who had died in the first year of the colonies' existence was Betty Bentley, an actress who had thought she was in competition with Brenda for lead actress status for decades. But movie goers, directors, and producers had always thought otherwise. It had been an act of selfless generosity that had prompted Brenda to offer a place at Curtain Call to Betty, which was repaid by Betty being one of a perpetually reconstituted quartet known as "The Terribles," whose sole function in the home was to criticize everything done there. Surprisingly, when Betty died, she left a considerable monetary gift to Curtain Call. Typically, though, it was left for the home "to do something nice for the residents at last."

The bequest money had finally come through in the late spring. Charlotte's suggestion was that they use the money to throw a truly memorable Christmas bash.

"That's a good idea," Brenda had said, "but I'm not sure how that would be that much better for the purpose of keeping their spirits up than any other Christmas party would be."

"What we could try is to research each resident and bring at least one person here to be with them over Christmas. Someone who can affirm their lives and give them a reason to live on," Charlotte had said. "I dare say that many who succumb at that time do so from the memories of what they've had, in contrast to the loneliness they feel now, because new friendships made at Curtain Call just don't make up for loved relatives and old friends they now are isolated from. The one thing that Betty kept saying that struck home with me was that perhaps we really should have established Curtain Call in Hollywood rather than here in rural Maryland, far from the context these folks lived in during their careers."

"All I ever heard from people I worked with in Hollywood," Brenda countered, "was how much they wanted to get out of the madness and just live quietly in the country for the rest of their lives."

"Which is really a pipe dream, isn't it?" Charlotte asked gently, touching Brenda's arm with her fingers from the need of the connection. "Look at us. You're back making a movie anytime you're asked (*White Orchid Found*) because of the obligations you feel to friends still in the business, and I have us off tracking down criminals (*Follow the Palm*) half the time. Most of us do want a deceleration of our lives, but not necessarily a total redirection of them."

"Something to think about," Brenda said. "Maybe the next time I win the Maryland lottery, I'll set up a retirement community near Hollywood. Maybe I'll learn from the mistakes being made here."

"What mistakes?" Charlotte asked. "I think you've been doing a bang-up job here."

"*We've* been doing a bang-up job," Brenda corrected. "The two of us together—well, the two of us plus a dedicated staff. But not doing so well in another area where I wanted to succeed. I wanted Curtain Call to become an integral part of this village—to revive the economy and to be something the locals valued and benefited from."

"They *have* benefited," Charlotte objected. "Curtain Call brings them business. You even put in shops at the entrance of the compound—the beauty and barber shops and a convenience store and gift shop—and are letting the local people operate there rent free."

"But we brought crime to the village and the village barber is dead because of us (*Follow the Palm*). And there are Joyce and Todd. They were already displeased with us, and now they're saying the guest house we're building will take business from them."

The Vales owned and operated a B&B from Joyce's ancestral home directly across the street from Brenda's house. The two had been classmates through high school, and Joyce always felt she had been in Brenda's shadow—and it didn't help relations at all when Joyce's daughter was swept up and killed in one of Charlotte's investigations (*By the Howling*).

It was true that there had already been other rocky times as well. A bitter rival of Brenda's had made Curtain Call a distribution point for drugs, and the village barber, whose wife was both the village beautician and town clerk, had died before Charlotte mobilized the authorities to close down the drug operation. But none of that was either

Brenda's or Curtain Calls' fault, and Charlotte was quick to tell Brenda that.

"And Joyce is more mad at me than you," she added. "Todd has always been more understanding. We can make the townspeople part of the plan, though. Just as you had originally planned, Curtain Call really is to their benefit. We can involve them in the Christmas celebrations and make it worth their while to be included. And, I've been thinking, we really don't want to have to run a guest house ourselves. We could just let the Vales run it as an adjunct of their B&B—and let them keep the profits. We just want there to be accommodations for those visiting our residents. And Todd's a gifted artist. We can ask him to paint Christmas-theme paintings that we'll use to decorate Curtain Call during Christmas and he can put price tags on them to sell them to residents and those coming in for Christmas."

And from this built the most elaborate part of the Curtain Call Christmas celebrations plan—tracking down and matching people from the residents' past who they would love to be with over Christmas and convincing them to come to Hopewell for Christmas at Curtain Call's expense.

It was a plan that was working out well, including bringing the Vales back into the fold—right up to Thanksgiving, when the marking of that day at Curtain Call nearly undid everything they were planning for Christmas.

* * * *

Where it started was probably the storm on November 20th that put the power out. The generator kicked on in the main building, but it didn't give full power. The lights were dim, which made the spirits of Curtain Call's residents dim too and forced the staff to go into overdrive in cheerfulness, an effort the residents always were able to see through—with the help of backbiting by The Terribles.

It had been raining for more than a week at that point, it was chilly and gloomy both inside and outside, and the generator was as deficient in providing full heat as it was in providing full lighting. The view of the surrounding river that was so verdant and jaunty in the spring, summer, and fall, looked bleak and foreboding in the winter. It was, after all, November. The generator was only needed for a few hours and then electricity kicked back on in the main building, but just that short time out set a gloomy atmosphere for the next week.

The primary power didn't come back on in some of the out buildings, though, including the large freezer in one of the storage buildings. This wasn't discovered until the next Tuesday, and only then when someone went to the freezer to retrieve the Thanksgiving turkeys to start the thawing process.

The turkeys, however, had thawed days earlier and now were beyond hope.

Brenda, Charlotte, and Evonne Clagett, the petite redheaded dynamo executive director of Curtain Call, were in a meeting in Evonne's office on Tuesday afternoon when a crestfallen Isaac, the head cook, came to them and reported that Thanksgiving dinner would be turkeyless. There wasn't another turkey to be had within a hundred miles of Hopewell. He had already tried that.

"The best we can do is carryout chicken," he said.

Evonne, always cheering and looking on the bright side, said, "There will be some who will see that as a treat and better than turkey."

"Yes, but The Terribles will make a big deal of there being no turkey and will gleefully stir up the others," Charlotte said, "even while they enjoy the chicken."

"They would have complained about the turkey anyway," Brenda said, and the women had a good laugh over the truth and irony that revealed.

But Isaac wasn't laughing, and Brenda noticed that. "That's not all of the bad news, is it, Isaac?" she said.

"No ma'am, it's not," he answered. "We've given a big buildup to there being homemade pumpkin ice cream for Thanksgiving dinner desert."

"And?" Charlotte asked.

"And, the ice cream was already made and was in the same freezer the turkeys were in."

"Then you'll just have to spin your usual magic, won't you, and come up with something the residents will see as equally impressive?" Evonne said.

"Yes, ma'am," Isaac answered, mollified by the praise Evonne had couched the bad news in—that he was still on the hook for Thanksgiving dinner desert. "'Course we're going to be right busy with the rest of the meal."

"Bea bakes a mean pie," Brenda said, referring to Brenda and Charlotte's housekeeper, Bea Helgerson (*What's the Point?*). "I'm sure she'd be happy to help with that."

It wasn't the best of solutions, but it looked good in theory. Unfortunately, it looked better in theory than it played out in practice.

The foul weather held out, an outage struck again on Thanksgiving afternoon, and the Thanksgiving dinner was eaten to the hum of the generator and dim light, augmented by candles. Evonne loudly exclaimed the lighting to be romantic, and The Terribles, in unison, more loudly declared the candlelight to be "the pits"—along with the greasy chicken—declaring the kitchen staff had dimmed the lights on purpose so that the residents couldn't see that the chicken was moldy. Even while other resident were saying they couldn't choose between the mince, pumpkin, and pecan pie, "they all look so good," The Terribles were asking where the pumpkin ice cream was they'd been promised and looking forward to for weeks.

When the generator died in the middle of dessert and Evonne only then, in the silence, tuned into the sneezing and coughing floating across the room, Curtain Call's on-call physician, Larry Stanton, was called in. Very shortly after arriving, he declared, "What you have here is a flu epidemic. I'm afraid all of the residents will need to be confined to their rooms and the entire facility put under quarantine."

Charlotte's response was a four-letter word beginning with an "S." Brenda's response was a sneeze.

Dr. Stanton turned to her and said, "And you too, Brenda. Off you go home and straight to bed. Don't leave the house until I say you can. I'll be along to give you medicine and instructions after I've finished here."

Evonne's response was a nearly perky, "Both of you run along. I'll hold the fort here—and continue with the Christmas celebration planning."

As Charlotte was walking Brenda home in the incessant chilly rain, her thoughts were stuck on how many residents were even going to be around for Christmas for celebrations that had been planned to have them still around after Christmas. She very carefully didn't relate these thoughts to Brenda, though, who was struggling mightily to maintain her usually sunny disposition.

* * * *

Over the next ten days Brenda was confined to her house and most of the time to her bed. The couple's dogs, the Siberian husky Sam and the Boxer Rocket, thought that having one of their mistresses in the bed for such a prolonged period was the best thing that could happen—second only to having both of them there, although when they both were there, they rarely had attention to give to the

125

dogs. Brenda, a woman who normally was perpetually on the move, didn't agree, although she gave the dogs the attention they craved. Both Sam and Rocket had come to the women as abandoned dogs. Sam was acquired because Charlotte was looking after the dog of neighbors who left for an archaeological dig and never made it there alive (*By the Howling*), and Rocket had been abandoned to Charlotte by the man who previously owned the land Curtain Call was located on and who had feigned his death and pulled a disappearing act (*Retired with Prejudice*). However acquired, the women and dogs were now connected as devoted family.

Charlotte's time was even more frustrating during this period. Even though the good news on the medical front at Curtain Call was that Dr. Stanton had pulled all of the residents through the bout with the flu without any losses, and although the Vales liked the idea of managing Curtain Call's guest house when it was completed, it was increasingly obvious that the guest house wouldn't be completed before Christmas. The primary culprit for this was the weather, which just wasn't settling down to providing enough clear days to get the work done on time.

Of the other village residents, only Billy Zirkel, one-time juvenile parolee and now half owner, with Brenda and Charlotte, of the village gas station and garage (*Curtain Call*), was devoting time to the Christmas program plan. He was arranging travel for some forty guests they were bringing in for Christmas with the Curtain Call residents. And, as enthusiastic as he was, he was encountering trouble in bookings because the continuous foul weather was cutting down on the flights being offered.

On top of that the party store Charlotte had contacted for decorations for the hall and corridors of the main building had sold out their Christmas decorations already and the store of the caterer that had been contracted to bake the Christmas goodies for the party had burned down and the caterer had gone out of business.

Charlotte had been wandering around muttering about a "cursed Christmas," while perky Evonne's cheery "everything will work out fine" was growing more dubious by the day. As the days got gloomier rolling into December, so did the prospects for the Christmas program.

"How cold is it out there?" Brenda asked when Charlotte came up to deliver her breakfast in bed on Sunday, December 6th.

"The river is freezing up," Charlotte answered. "It's the first time I've known it to do that here."

"And how are the plans going for the Christmas celebrations at Curtain Call?"

"They're going along pretty well," Charlotte said, hedging. She hadn't burdened Brenda with how bad the plans had been going.

"You can't fib with me, Charlotte," Brenda said. "Thanks for trying, but I can tell they aren't going well. Tell me how bad it is."

Charlotte did just that, unburdening herself of all of the problems and stone walls she and Evonne had encountered over the past week and a half.

"I can see that it's time for me to get out of bed and go to work then," Brenda said. "I'm feeling fine now. And it's been bleaker than this. Remember last Christmas when we were getting married?"

"Do I," Charlotte said, with a laugh. "Snow up to our keisters at the church, our limousine being stolen from in front of the church, the difficulty in getting to the pier in Baltimore through the snow for our honeymoon cruise—and then the fire on board and the pirates (*Horrible Honeymoon*). And the Christmas before that with the robberies and murder on that Christmas market Rhine cruise we took with Marilyn and Chance (*An Inconsiderate*

Death). God, we've had some horrible Christmases together so far, haven't we?"

"No, they've been glorious, because we've had each other," Brenda answered.

Charlotte leaned over and kissed her, feeling that, with Brenda just being Brenda, the plans for this Christmas had now hit bottom and could only be going up.

As if to accentuate that, both dogs went up on their haunches in the bed, pricked up their ears, and gave little woofs. At that moment the doorbell rang down in the foyer. Giving Brenda another quick kiss and remarking that it must be friend rather than foe based on the dogs' behavior, Charlotte went downstairs and opened the door.

There, on the stoop, she found her brother, Chance, a Williamsburg physician, and his wife, Marilyn, a Methodist minister.

"Chance. Marilyn," Charlotte exclaimed in surprise. "We were just talking about you and the infamous Rhine River cruise."

"We heard about this fancy shindig you all are running for Christmas at the retirement home," Chance said. "Evonne tells us you are bringing in special loved ones for the festivities. I know we're early, but—"

"Evonne called you?" Charlotte asked, confused and not too quick on the uptake, "about the loved ones we're bringing in are for the residents?"

"Well," Chance persisted, "Evonne also said you were being run down enough by glitches in the planning for the party that you could qualify for being one of the old folks in the home."

"Now, Chance," Marilyn said, laying a hand on his arm. "Evonne said no such thing. And you called her to find out if there were problems here."

"Yes, we accept. We need you," Charlotte said, with a laugh, throwing the door all the way open. Chance and Marilyn Diamond indeed had been accompanying Charlotte and Brenda on many of their adventures (*An Inconvenient Death*, *Horrible Honeymoon*, *Fowler's Folly*) and had been a great help each time. And she wasn't about to turn down reinforcements now.

As they bustled in from the cold, Charlotte coughed. And for the first time she was fully cognizant that she had awakened this morning with a scratchy throat.

The arrival of the Diamonds indeed marked the beginning of an upswing in the planning. Soon after they arrived, Billy Zirkel called. "I hope I haven't overstepped. I was in Ocean City yesterday and happened on a party store that still had Christmas decorations. Now they don't. We have them. I hope that's OK."

"That's perfect," Charlotte said. "Thanks muchly. Can you drop them over to Evonne at Curtain Call?"

Next was Todd Vale. "Charlotte, I really don't think the guest house is going to be finished to house the people coming in for this Christmas party. I hope you don't mind that I've canvassed the village and I think we can manage rooms for them all with everyone pitching in."

"Just what we'd hoped," Charlotte said. "Thanks a million, Todd. Tell everyone that we'll pay them hotel prices."

"Everyone says that's not necessary, Charlotte—that they all want to help out."

"Thanks again. I couldn't have gotten a better Christmas present. It's the relationship with the village that Brenda has been hoping for. And say hi and a thank-you to Joyce too from Brenda and me. I know she's been helping you do this."

Following this was a call from Evonne. "Billy was just here dropping off party supplies and told me the airlines are dropping flights because of the weather. Just for insurance, I called out to Hollywood to Aaron Wooldridge, Brenda's long-time movie producer (*Coast to Coast*, *White Orchid Found*). He'd told me to let him know if Curtain Call

129

needed anything. I told him about the transportation problem and knew he had access to private planes. He couldn't weigh in fast enough that he loved the idea and, if he got an invitation to the party, he'd see that everyone on the guest list got flown into Baltimore. He said the residents of Curtain Call were all his people too—movie people— and that he'd been trying to think up a way he could help financially with the retirement home. I hope I didn't—"

"Evonne, you're an absolute angel. We should have invited him from the get go—and the director, Howard Holton, too (*Coast to Coast*, *White Orchid Found*). You're a doll for backstopping us on that."

As she rang off, the doorbell sounded again. Half way to the door, Charlotte had a coughing fit, which produced a frown—an expression that evaporated when she opened the door.

"Zenna!" Charlotte exclaimed, looking up and down the street, pulling the former owner of Zenna's Russian Bakery in the village into the house, and shutting the door. "You shouldn't be here."

She apparently hadn't come just for a cup of tea. She had a suitcase with her.

"I'm sure it's safe to come now," Zenna said. She had been a spy for the United States in her native Russia and had been salted away here in Hopewell. The Russians had found her and she'd received a new identity and been moved up the coast to Chestertown. She hadn't been back to Hopewell since (*Retired with Prejudice*, *Curtain Call*).

"I come to help. You have housekeeper who is good baker, yes?"

"Yes, Bea Helgerson. But I don't understand."

"You throw party at retirement home, yes?"

"Yes, but—"

"And place where you ordered Christmas cookies and cakes for it burned down, yes?"

"Yes."

"Well, I'm here to do the baking you need—maybe with this Bea Helgerson, if she want to help."

"That would be wonderful, Zenna. You're a life saver. I'm sure Bea wants to help; she's already said she'd do anything she could to help," Charlotte said. "You can stay with us. We'll see that no one knows you're here."

Everything was back on the road now. There was only one negative thing Charlotte had to report when she went back up to Brenda and her bedroom, where Brenda was holding court with Marilyn and Chance—and the pups.

"You said this was the day you could get out of bed, Brenda," Charlottes said, as she entered the room. "Then I'm afraid that you'll have to vacate and turn the bed over to me. I think it's my turn with the flu."

* * * *

Prospects were looking up for the Christmas festivities at Curtain Call for the next ten days. Plans were falling into place. It was like someone up there was looking out for them after all.

Charlotte didn't have the flu; she was just run down from the concern of little working out right up to that point and with Brenda having the flu. It was just a head cold that was gone in a week. Chance and Marilyn were a big help, and their presence, as always, was both calming and helped to bring humor back into the process, which had been challenged because the usual cheerleaders were Evonne and Brenda. Evonne had been stretched to her limits— everyone being surprised that the woman actually had limits—and Brenda had been physically miserable and separated from everyone but Charlotte.

"It's always good to have both a doctor and a minister in the house" was a greeting Charlotte used whenever she opened to the door to her brother and sister-in-law. She found that to be a truism, and is was just as true

131

in the current circumstance. Bea and Zenna were getting along famously and turning out the most tantalizing savories and sweets for the party. Evonne—a constant blessing herself and having gotten a second wind when the problems began turning around—had shipped in another generator, which was hooked up to the storage building with the extra freezers in it. So, there was little chance now that what Bea and Zenna were stashing away for finishing off later would be ruined.

The Vales had assigned housing in the village for all of the visitors expected to come from out of town. And the movie connections of many of these folks had put stars in the eyes of the villagers and made them even more welcoming of visitors at Christmas. There even was a slight chance that the guest house would be finished in time—the furniture for it was in a warehouse in Baltimore, just waiting to be put on trucks. The residents of Curtain Call were being enlisted to help decorate Curtain Call for Christmas, and, all but The Terribles, who were grousing when someone was looking but putting another ball on the gigantic tree in the day room when they didn't think anyone was watching, were having a ball. They weren't thinking of their infirmities and, only in moments of weakness, were worrying about surviving into the new year.

Although the residents were told about the party, set for the afternoon of Christmas Eve, and nearly all that was planned for it, and were told that there was a special surprise, they weren't told that the surprise was that each of them would have at least one "best friend" visitor from the party through New Years. Evonne and Dr. Stanton had agreed that telling them of this beforehand would excite them too much. The downside was that The Terribles spent the time throwing out all sorts of disgusting possibilities of what the "surprise" would be, and the other residents—and certainly Evonne's staff—got a little excitable about this razzing.

And it was good they hadn't made promises on the surprise, because on Friday, the 18th, the weather asserted itself again. It began to snow that night. It came down so fast and furiously that the pastor of Charlotte and Brenda's church, Don Dunkel, canceled church services on Sunday. This had almost never happened before. He did, though, trudge to Curtain Call in the snow and hold services there, with the singing of Christmas carols.

The snow continued into the week. When Billy Zirkel delivered fuel for the generators on Monday, he warned that that was all he had on hand at the village's gas station and that everyone should pray that the electricity didn't go out village wide for any length of time. He possibly should have suggested that this hope be covered in prayers on Sunday, the previous, day, because the electricity did go out Monday night. He'd told Evonne he thought the generators could run on what they had for two days, thus until sometime on the 23rd. The party was on the 24th. He'd also dropped the ominous news that, if the snow didn't stop, the Easton airport would have to be closed down. That's where Aaron Woolridge's private jets, delivering the visitors, were set to land. And even if they could land there, Easton was a long drive, over snow-covered roads, from Hopewell.

Tuesday morning, Evonne called the gas station to try to find out from Billy about obtaining more fuel for the generators, which now were carrying the burden at Curtain Call. But no one answered his phone.

In the dim light and slight chill of the Curtain Call day room, more and more heed was being taken of the scenarios of disaster being spun and proclaimed by The Terribles, who took up position at the center of the room. Perhaps more damage was being done and depression was being spread by Hortense Fowler, resident and self-proclaimed fortuneteller, who set herself up at a table in a quiet corner, and, as she always was prone to do, gleefully served a good many bored and depressed residents fortunes foretelling their immediate demise during Christmas week.

A nurse's aide discovered her, and she was whisked away to her suite, but not before she had spread considerable consternation and panic. This was an oft-played scene at Curtain Call. Like some of the other residents, in addition to readily predicting the demise of compatriots at the retirement home, Hortense openly showed satisfaction whenever someone passed on that it hadn't been her.

On the evening of 23 December, it had stopped snowing, but the white stuff was some four feet deep outside. Bea and Zenna were in the kitchen at Curtain Call, bundled up and trudging a path between storage buildings and the Curtain Call kitchen and pulling what they'd prepared out of the storage room freezers to go ahead and get it thawed or baked, as appropriate, while there still was generator power. Brenda, Charlotte, the Diamonds, and Evonne were also at Curtain Call, preparing to shut down the generator to the storage room and transfer whatever fuel was left there to the main generator. They, and the staff members who had managed to make it through the snow from the staff apartments at the end of Spring Street, were also collecting blankets and candles and distributing them to the suites—Evonne letting them know which residents couldn't be given candles for fear they'd burn the place down. Staff members were setting up a roster for sitting with these residents in their rooms to monitor the candles.

They worked quickly, anticipating that the generator would cough and die at any moment.

At midnight on the eve of Christmas Eve, with all of the residents tucked in bed, but everyone else still on the premises, preparing for the worst—at the nadir of their experience and expectations—their world started brightening up once more.

A whirring and grinding sound cut through the silence of the snow-covered night. Evonne went to the front door of Curtain Call and turned on the porch lights. Approaching, through the snow, was a snowplow, driven by Billy Zirkel, with Don Dunkel, dressed as Santa Claus, rising up over the roof of the cab and waving his arms.

A supply of fuel for the generators had arrived. Also being delivered was more good news from Billy.

"We passed crews working on the lines," He informed the group gathering in the foyer. "They know there's a retirement home down here, and they promise to have the electricity back up today."

"You're an angel," Evonne said, reaching out to hug him.

"You both are," Brenda said. "We couldn't have done any of this without you."

"There's more," Don Dunkel said, "and more because of Billy. We're just the first snowplow. Billy services the snowplows for the county. Sheriff Haws and Deputy Burch, and a bunch of snowplow workers are coming behind us with every snowplow in the county."

"My goodness, what for?" Evonne asked.

"Your guests," Billy answered. "Your friend's jets got them to the international airport in Baltimore, which is still open, and Ms. Diamond's friend from her old FBI office in Annapolis got them on tug boats to cross the bay to Easton, which is about as far up the Choptank as the river is cleared. Snowplows are bringing them the rest of the way."

So, the residents of Curtain Call woke up to the smells of Christmas wafting from the kitchens, long-unseen special personal friends, and a horde of new friends coming in from the village or driving snowplows.

The happy spirits that ruled the day would have been enough to spoil the fun of The Terribles, if the atmosphere of good will hadn't been enough to sweep them up in the festivities as well.

On the last arriving plow, Brenda received her best Christmas present. She was urged to go to the door to welcome the plow to find that it carried her son, the Hollywood star Tony Trice, and his fiancée, the pro tennis player Michelle Minor (*Retired with Prejudice, Coast to Coast, White Orchid Found, Curtain Call*). When Brenda was able to calm herself, she turned to Charlotte and said, in a choked voice, "No one told me."

"I racked my brain trying to come up with a Christmas gift for you, Brenda, but you have everything. We were bringing in someone for all of the residents, and Chance and Marilyn came in for me. So, we brought Tony and Michelle in for you."

"You couldn't have come up with a better present," Brenda said, tears in her eyes. "And I'll have a present for you later—at home."

"I'm looking forward to it. You light up my life."

As if on cue, the electricity came on.

Needless to say, the plan for a special Christmas for the residents of Curtain Call worked a charm. And afterward, when those who made it possible were savoring their success with mulled wine in the merry shambles of the day room and started bringing up all of the obstacles they'd had to overcome, Pastor Dunkel wrapped it up for them. "Overcoming problems has made it all the more worthwhile," he said. "That could be said to be the Christmas message—the Christ star shining through adversity. I heard someone say that these Christmas plans had been cursed. If so, I say they were blessedly cursed. It's a Christmas none of us will forget—and one that all of us can be proud we were a part of."

As far as the basic purposes of all of this when Brenda and Charlotte came up with the concept, the two were sure that they had solidified the village and retirement home relations and they had nearly been successful in keeping the ghost of death from the homes doors for the season. Only one resident of Curtain Call died during Christmas week—Hortense Fowler, the fortuneteller who had made a practice of gleefully forecasting the deaths of all the other residents. She died peacefully in her sleep on Boxing Day. She was 104 and had been the only resident not to have caught the flu at Thanksgiving.

~

About the Author

Olivia Stowe is a published author under different names and in other dimensions of fiction and nonfiction and lives quietly in a university town with an indulgent spouse.

Olivia is at www.CyberworldPublishing.com.

Our authors like to receive feedback and appreciate reviews being posted at distributor and review sites.

Olivia's Books

All Olivia's, except the "Bundles," are available in paperback and e-book.

Mystery Romance
Restoring the Castle
Final Flight

The Charlotte Diamond mystery series
By The Howling (Book 1)
Retired with Prejudice (Book 2)
Coast to Coast (Book 3)
An Inconvenient Death (Book 4)
What's The Point? (Book 5)
White Orchid Found (Book 6)
Curtain Call (Book 7)
Horrid Honeymoon (Book 8)
Follow the Palm (Book 9)
Fowler's Folly (Book 10
Making Room at Christmas (Seasonal Special)
Cassandra's last Spotlight (Seasonal Special)
Blessedly Cursed Christmas (Seasonal Special)
Charlotte Diamond Mysteries Bundle 1 (Books 1&2)
Charlotte Diamond Mysteries Bundle 2 (Books 3&4)
Charlotte Diamond Mysteries Bundle 3 (Books 5&6)

The Savannah Series
Chatham Square
Savannah Time

Olivia's Inspirational Christmas collections
Christmas Seconds (2011)
Spirit of Christmas (2010)